Nephilim Code

Nova

By TP Hogan

National Library of Australia Cataloguing-in-Publication entry

Hogan, T.P., author.
    Nova / TP Hogan.
    ISBN: 9780992587628 (paperback)
    Hogan, T.P. Nephilim Code ; book 1.
    For young adults.
    Angels--Fiction. Paranormal fiction.
A823.4

Acknowledgements

Wow, what a ride this story has been. There are so many people who helped me along the way with encouragement, assisting with research, accepting the role of sounding board (not that some of you had much choice), and keeping me sane when my characters were sending me mental. Thank you to you all. There are just too many to name.

A special thanks to my Mum for letting me use her house as a writers retreat, and being there at all hours to talk about the story as though it, and the characters were real.

As always, a special thanks to my husband who put up with Nephilim invading our supposed 'alone time', and who re-arranged our house so I could have more space for post-it-notes and whiteboards. Without your support, assistance and research skills, 'Nephilim Code' would have just stayed in the box of ideas.

Chapter One

Grabbing my camera, I escaped to the cool night air of the rooftop. With a quick glance to judge the state of the cement tiles, I decided I wasn't going land in a puddle of water and the filth wasn't too bad for the knees of my jeans and knelt at the balustrade. The concrete wall was the perfect height to rest my camera as I slowly swept the familiar view through the lens. Automatically, I adjusted the focus to take in the details. The rain from earlier had left the streets glimmering under the electric lights and the council's strands of lights snaking the tree trunks turned it into a fairy wonderland. It was empty. Not surprising really; it was nearly midnight.

Reaching the end of the street, I smiled. Right on the edge of blue and pink neon reflecting in the puddles, a guy in a greasy apron leaned against the wall. He had a knee cocked with his foot resting on the stone behind him and one hand held a cigarette. He couldn't have been more perfect if I'd posed him myself. With a flick of my finger, I turned the flash off. It would be useless from this distance. I couldn't see the guy's face but his body was slender and trim.

Hopefully, I could get in a few good shots before he moved.

Flicking the butt, he walked into the night. I twisted the lens to keep him in focus, to no avail. The street was back to being empty. Normally something interesting caught my attention. I simply had to stay still long enough.

I jumped with a gasp as, behind me, the roof door slammed opened and two men ran to the other side. Curiously, I watched them. They didn't appear to have seen me, but then I'd automatically knelt slightly in the shadows to shield the lens from the glare of the security light. They were both in silhouette but one was noticeably taller than the other.

"You still haven't told me what they said."

That was the shorter one speaking. He was in just enough light for me to see he had a brown jacket which looked like a throwback to the early 1900's, when they wore them as aviator uniforms.

"I know where he is and I'm getting him out of there."

The taller one had a slight American twang. Not so thick it sounded like I was watching a blockbuster, but enough that my ears picked up on it.

"I'm coming with you."

I frowned as the man in brown turned his back on the taller one. The man in the darkness slid his arms under the arms of the guy in brown, linked his hands on his wrists and lifted off.

I'm not kidding. The man in silhouette lifted off the rooftop. He flew. Within seconds he was overhead then gone. My heart pounded and I reminded myself to breathe as I stared up at the empty sky. Blinking, I quickly looked back across the roof. It wasn't an illusion. Both men had disappeared. The roof was empty. There was no film crew, no wires or special effects. I was not watching a movie. I hadn't fallen asleep. He flew.

"Holy Mother of…" I breathed as I glanced down at the camera in my hands. I had my finger on the shutter. For about five seconds I knelt there on the rooftop, frozen. Then I hurriedly raced to my unit. I fumbled at my retractable belt clip for my swipe card as the roof door closed behind me. Yanking the camera strap from around my neck, I quickly caught my front door before it slammed. I didn't need to wake Kate or Clancy. Grumpy and tired flat mates were not high on my list of priorities right now. Not even bothering with the light switch, I headed straight for my studio as I undid the catch for the memory card.

"Come on, come on, come on," I told my computer as it booted.

Even in my excitement I was careful to place my camera in its bag as I waited for the computer screen to show the familiar logo-ed wallpaper. I wasn't made of money and it wasn't worth a busted camera even if I'd managed to capture him…*bloody hell*…flying.

Shoving the keyboard onto the edge of my monitor stand, I grabbed my stylus and ran it across the pad, navigating the programs. Out of habit I opened a new file, named it with today's date and copied the photos across. As the little man in the computer worked on that small task, I opened up the file on the memory card and scrolled to the last lot of photos.

"Both men…man in brown turning around…and…damn."

I shoved my free hand through my hair. The last shot was of the two men with their feet firmly on the ground. It looked like the guy in the shadows was giving the other guy the Heimlich manoeuvre. Although… I tapped the little magnifying glass a few times then centred onto the face of the man in darkness. In the very last shot he was looking up, as if to see where he was going. As you do. When you're about to fly. In this one shot, his face was caught in the wash from the security light. The zoom of the camera worked against me and the close up was too grainy. Transferring the photo to my editing suite, I slid the scribe pad into my lap, hit the tilt on my chair and planted my feet on the edge of the desk. Perhaps, not the most ergonomic set up, but it was the most comfortable way for me to work. With my bottom lip between my teeth, I used the program to clean up the zoom. Waiting for the render between each clean up nearly killed me. After four renders, with each pass becoming clearer and clearer, it was almost four in the morning. I had a shoot at eight, but there was no way on God's green earth I was going to give up on this. Finally I had a clean shot…and a clear look at his face. My feet hit the floor and I grabbed the scribe pad to keep it from sliding off my lap. My mouth hung open as I stared.

"No beeping way," I breathed. "You've got to be kidding me."

The mystery Superman was none other than my new neighbour. He'd moved into the Rainne's old place, one flat to the left and across the hallway, about four weeks ago. We hadn't been officially introduced but I'd passed him a few times in the hall. Kate had more than enough to say about him. Apparently he was quite the gentleman. He'd been around here to fix the sink and a shelf, and had thus far remained free from adding to the notches on her bedpost. I hadn't even bothered to ask why she hadn't gone to the Body Corporate about the maintenance. He fit the Superman profile all right. Six-two, dark hair, laser blue eyes, a body most girls would love to get their hands on…and he could fly.

This 'Clark Kent' didn't wear glasses as far as I'd seen and his name was Zeph Angelis.

Chapter Two

Mrs Kendrick answered my knock on her front door.

"Hey, Mrs K, it's 'be nice to your neighbour day'." I grinned, holding up two plastic shopping bags; the sixteen takeaway containers inside. "Not a single mushroom in sight, so Sally should be happy."

Mrs Kendrick gave an embarrassed smile but I could see the relief in her eyes. "I told you last month you didn't need to do this, Nova."

"I know." I shrugged. "But you know me, come the full moon and I hit 'Master Chef' mode. Can't help myself."

She opened the door wider. "Sally wanted to give you something. Would you come in?"

"Sure."

Sally was at the computer in the lounge room but she catapulted herself at me as soon as she saw I was there.

I pulled away enough to wave at her. Grabbing my hand, she pulled me to the kitchen.

"I ma sis fa oo," she told me.

"I made this for you." Mrs K translated.

Sally took a biscuit tin off the bench and opened it before thrusting it at me. Peering inside, I saw about six iced biscuits. They were round and iced in yellow with black smiley faces. The icing was smooth and near perfect.

"Wow. For me?" I didn't know '*Wow*', but I signed '*For me?*' My grasp of Auslan was very, very basic, but Mrs K and Sally had taught me a few words.

"Ya." Sally spoke as she signed then selected one of the biscuits and handed it to me.

It was actually very good. I overdramatised my enjoyment of it which made her laugh.

"Did you make these yourself?"

Sally's eyes flicked behind me as her mum obviously translated, and she nodded.

"Good." I signed as I spoke.

Replacing the lid, she passed the tin over to me.

"*All?*" I had my mouth full and signed the one handed question.

"Aw."

"*Thank you.*"

She squeezed me in a hug then pointed to the living room. "Omrurk."

"I told her, if she finished her homework by six I would take her for an ice cream," Mrs K told me as Sally dashed off into the other room.

"Fair enough. I've got to go, too." I held up my last two shopping bags. "Almost done."

"Nova?" I stopped at the door.

Mrs K took the door from my hand and held it open behind me. "Thank you. I'm sure there are more deserving people who need your kindness…but thank you."

"Welcome. See ya."

I left their flat feeling like a million bucks. Contrary to what Clancy said on a regular basis, I wasn't on some sort of crusade to save all the down-and-outers single handed. Mrs Turek on the first floor barely had any visitors and didn't get out much, Mr Allens on the third floor was in a wheelchair and Mr Kendrick had been deployed to Afghanistan on his third tour. A few home cooked meals wasn't going to rescue them from their hardships. I was glad no one had questioned me about the fourth load of meals. Hopefully they hadn't actually noticed.

I stood at the door, my heart pounding. Taking a slow breath, I tried to lift my hand but baulked. This was silly. I shouldn't be so nervous. Superman was a nice alien. Shaking my head at my own stupidity, I took a step back and knocked purposefully. The sound seemed to echo in the room behind the door and no one answered. Trying again another two times gained the same result. Obviously no one was home, or someone was pretending not to be. With a shrug, I ignored my disappointment and embraced my relief as I headed for the elevator. Honestly, I had no idea what I was going to say to Zeph anyway.

Lost in my own thoughts, I only realised I still had the bags of food when on the footpath. I now had to go all the way back upstairs. Thank goodness for a working elevator. Turning to go back, I noticed movement at the brick fencing which cordoned off the bins for the units.

"Hey, Mr Wendel." I called out as I walked towards him.

I had no idea what his real name was, but the name from the song suited him. He'd never complained.

"Missy Quinn." He gave a quick nod then resumed pawing through the bins.

I tried not to react to the smell. The bins weren't so bad. It was him. Strong BO, oily hair, old unwashed clothes and rank sweat was not a good combination.

"Where are you staying these days?" I watched him toss a few cans into his trolley.

"Varine, but the walls wanted to touch. Can't let them."

"You hungry?"

"Tummy goes ping."

Taking that as a yes, I pulled out one of the meals. "Homemade for someone who wasn't home. It's yours if you want it."

Mr Wendel leaned towards me and sniffed the air like a dog at the wind. With a vigorous nod he shuffled towards me, clinking as he moved. Snatching the plastic container from my hand, he scurried back to his original distance as if he was afraid I'd change my mind. From somewhere in the depths of his clothes he pulled out a pocket knife and wiped the spoon implement with the side of his fingerless glove before cracking open the lid and chowing down.

"I haven't seen you in a while." I hauled myself onto the ledge of the brick barrier. I couldn't tell how old he was under the long, lanky hair and heavy beard. There wasn't much grey in the strands, but he moved at a shuffle and his voice sounded older. I guessed him to be late forties, early fifties…maybe.

Shaking his head, he continued to inhale the stew. "Talked to the stars. I saw what you saw." He took half a step towards me and nodded. "High up."

My thoughts immediately went to my flying neighbour, but that couldn't be right.

"Excuse me?"

Wiping his hand across his mouth, Mr Wendel made a 'chika' noise, then repeated it several times in quick succession, before pointing to my camera.

"You saw it. I saw it. High on Arden."

Understanding dawned as I realised he meant my photo which was used in an advertisement billboard on Arden street. "How did you know it was my photo?"

He shrugged. Or at least I think he did. It was a little hard to tell with his many layers of clothes. He went back to making the 'chika' noise between the last mouthfuls. I don't think I'd ever seen anyone eat so fast, but then, I had no idea when his last meal was.

"I've got to go." I jumped down from the brick work. "I've got to meet some friends."

Mr Wendel breathed in and made a move toward me like he wanted something. With hesitant jerky movements he pointed to the plastic bags still at my side. "I have…friends."

I watched him look down at the ground and shuffle before stealing a quick glance back at me.

"They won't last more than a few hours out of the fridge." I warned him.

He nodded. I really didn't want to be responsible if he got food poisoning, but if he really did have homeless friends who were as hungry as he was…well, we didn't need the meals that much. Giving a casual salute, I pushed away from the wall.

"See you around, Mr Wendel."

He didn't move from where he was. "God bless you, Missy Quinn."

Walking away from the bins, I heard the rustle of the plastic bags. When I glanced back he was trundling away in the opposite direction with his trolley half full of cans and the bags were gone.

As I walked down the street I could still clearly remember the first time I'd met him. I'd been new to the city and hadn't taken note of where I was when I was taking photos. Completely lost, I was beginning to panic when he came out of an alleyway tapping his head. "Tell me point B."

"Excuse me?"

He tapped his head again. "Map. It doesn't work without an A and B."

It took me a few seconds to realise this homeless man had figured out I was lost. "Were you watching me?"

"Watching you watching the world." He looked up at the sky with a smile. "But you forgot to look at your feet."

"My feet?"

Giving a low chuckle, he ran his fingers over his beard. "But now the breadcrumbs are gone. But I've got stones."

He was strange and he stank to high heaven but he kept his distance and didn't seem threatening.

"Okay, I need to get to Prowden Hotel."

It wasn't where I was staying but I knew my way from there.

"Poor Dorothy. You are a long way from home. But I can find the yellow." His smile was kind of shy.

"My name's not…oh, right, Wizard of Oz, got you. You like fairy tales?"

"Fairies don't have tails."

That made me laugh. "How do you know, have you seen one?"

The way he rubbed his nose and shook his head reminded me of Leonardo DiCaprio in '*What's eating Gilbert Grape?*'.

"Can't tell. They'll be upset if I did."

The walk to the hotel took about forty-five minutes at the shuffling pace he set, and the conversation rambled down some strange rabbit holes along the way. I'd seen Mr Wendel off and on over the past few years and I didn't know much more about him than that first day. As far as I could tell he was harmless. Homeless and penniless, but harmless. He also had a tendency to talk in riddles. Being part of the fringes of society would do that to a person.

"Earth to Nova."

"Huh?" I looked up at the snap of Clancy's fingers. I'd walked the entire way to Labyrinth in what felt like a few minutes. It was a half-hour walk. "Hi, Clancy. Fancy meeting you here."

Rolling his eyes, he pushed open the door and let me enter first. I breathed in deeply the scent of freshly brewed coffee and old books as I stepped inside. Although eBooks might be doing away with paper books, you wouldn't know it here. Steampunk-esque with owls made of cogs, mannequins sporting the hoops of old skirts and metal butterfly wings mingled in the walkways with dark leather chairs, and four-foot globes. The second-hand-bookshop-come-coffee-shop was one of a kind.

I waved at Kate and she tossed a smile back from behind the coffee machine. Her hair was shorter than it had been yesterday morning when I'd last seen her, and flicked out like a demented halo around her head. It also sported about sixteen shades of red. Obviously she'd let Clancy have free rein on it again.

He claimed our usual table and slid into the wingback leather chair before I could.

"Snoozer loser." He quipped.

"If you were a gentleman –."

"I'm charming, my dear, not sincere."

I made a face at him as I placed the camera bag on the table and pulled away the horrid straight backed wooden Victorian style chair. I swapped it for a second wingback chair, only this one was red with black velvet paisley running over it.

"Much better." Hooking the strap of the camera bag around my leg, I tucked it under the chair as I sat.

Clancy had slid his arms across the table and opened his mouth to speak but he suddenly pulled back, crossed his arms over his chest and dropped his head to stare at his lap. His defensive posture made me look up.

The waitress was obviously new and was staring at Clancy with her mouth dropped open in shock.

"It's okay," I told her. "We're Kate's regulars, she'll have the order."

"Uh-huh." She grunted.

"Take a photo, it'll last longer." Clancy bit out.

The waitress blinked as if only now realising she was being rude. "Kate, sure. Right. I'll leave you to it then."

He sighed heavily as she hurried away. "You'd think I'd be used to it by now."

"Being checked out by cute girls? I doubt it. At least I hope not."

It was strange. I'd known Clancy nearly four years and I didn't saw his scars anymore. Not until it was pointed out like that. It was amazing that something as obvious as burn scars to thirty percent of his body could be overlooked so easily. Perhaps it was because he usually wore long pants and long sleeves or perhaps I'd known him so long I was used to them.

He gave me a pointed look then twitched a smile at my teasing. "Enough about me, what's going on in that head of yours?"

"Nothing."

"Why do I not believe you?"

I sighed. "Other than the wedding tonight and the schools for the next three weeks, I have no special project."

"Uh-huh, that's why you were up to goodness knows when last night, muttering and pacing out in your studio."

"I woke you?"

He shrugged. "I was awake already, I came out for a drink."

I glanced down at the cogs under the resin of the table, tracing one of them with a fingernail. This was my chance to tell him what I'd seen, but I hesitated. I couldn't think of one possible way to explain it without seeming cuckoo. I didn't have the evidence and even if he believed me, he'd think I'd dreamed it or something.

"What do you think of our new next door neighbour?"

"The one Kate's panting after?"

It was my turn to give him a look. "That's crude."

"But true." Kate quipped as she placed two cups with saucers on the table between us. "Nova, one regular latte and for Clancy, a decaf skinny soy latte with a sugar substitute. AKA…the pointless."

Kate had a mongrel accent, the result of having a French father, a German mother and growing up in Australia. As a result, my name in her mouth always sounded like *Noo-fear*. I loved it.

She placed her hands on her hips. "And if you ask me, I think he is just delicious."

It took me a moment to realise she hadn't given the coffee a gender. She was answering my question.

"I know you think he's hot, but what do you actually know about him."

"Good with his hands." She winked.

"Kate, I'm serious."

Glancing around the near empty coffee area she dragged that horrid chair back to our table and planted herself in it. "He came here looking for his brother."

That could explain the 'he', mentioned last night. I felt the heat from my mug nearly burn my fingers and adjusted my grip. "From where?"

"USA I'd assume from his accent."

Clancy snorted. "Kate, you've got an accent and you were born here."

"I don't have an accent."

"What else?" I asked before their bickering could start. Honestly, the way these two carried on sometimes, you'd think they were siblings.

Kate placed her elbow on the table and rested her chin in her hand. "That's about it."

"So he could be a serial killer and we'd been none the wiser."

"I'm sure we'll find out soon enough," Clancy agreed as he took a sip of his swill.

"He could be like Dexter, then he'd be a good serial killer."

"Dexter?" I couldn't place the name.

Clancy rolled his eyes. "TV show, forget it."

I wasn't surprised. Kate could be watching up to eight TV shows concurrently and still not mix up any of the characters or plot lines. It was a wonder she had any time for her study or her job, but somehow she managed it.

Kate twisted in her seat and patted my leg. "I know, why don't you pretend he's one of your strays and invite him around for dinner?"

"My strays?"

"Come on." Clancy laughed. "Don't play innocent. You're like the Pied Piper. I'm surprised they don't literally follow you down the street."

I took a slow sip of my coffee. My dad had always given money to beggars and taken some home for a cooked meal. Somewhere along the way I'd picked up the habit. Being female, I played it safe by inviting neighbours and people I'd known a while over for dinner, not complete strangers. Inviting Superman for a meal? Well, it didn't get any stranger than that.

"That's not such a bad idea."

Chapter Three

There is quite a difference between planning something and the execution thereof. One of the stepping stones to having Zeph Angelis come for dinner was to actually issue the invitation. That minor detail eluded us, as did the man in question. Despite our attempts, we didn't see him that day or the next. On the Monday, Kate thought she heard music from inside his flat, but no one answered her knock. I was actually in two minds about the outcome. Okay, more than two. I wanted to ask him about what I saw him do. How he did it, what it felt like, when did he first discover he could, how did he navigate…that sort of thing. I didn't know how to ask or even if I should. That led to other thoughts. No normal human could fly, which meant he either wasn't normal…or wasn't human. Superman was an alien. Zeph could be one too, or a robot, or a government experiment…well, he did have an American accent, it was possible. One thing for sure, it was doubtful I could ask in front of Kate or Clancy. I certainly did not want to ask while I was on my own with him. I'd seen more than enough

movies, thank you. A move like that could be
disadvantageous to my health.

With my mind spinning like a merry-go-round that
wouldn't stop, I took my camera and my watering can
up to the roof. Humming to myself in an attempt to
keep my mind free from latching onto the Superman
saga all over again, I went to my little herb shelter
and came to a sudden halt. I knew I'd neglected them
since Thursday last week, and the last time we'd had
rain was Friday. Yet they were wet. As if someone
had watered them. The ground wasn't sopping, but it
was damp under the shelter.

Nobody had ever bothered to touch my plants
before. They'd almost died the time I went to Cairns
for two weeks. Slowly, I backed out of the greenery
and stepped around the slight corner to my bench
seat. I felt a little like the three bears returning home
from the day in the woods.

Someone's been on my roof.

Someone's been watering my plants.

And now someone was sleeping on my bench seat.

He had one leg bent with his knee resting on the
back of the seat while the other one stretched out
along it. One hand rested on his stomach and the
other lay near his shoulder as the crook of his elbow
shielded his eyes. The sun was now on the ground,
and if he'd been shading his eyes then he'd been
asleep for about half an hour or so. He was in jeans
and a long sleeved, white shirt with the sleeves
pushed up a little to show muscular forearms. I wasn't
sure how he stayed balanced on the beam of the seat.
It wasn't a very big bench…and he was extremely
broad. From the looks of it, all muscle.

Very carefully, I set the watering can on the ground and brought my camera around. I would need him to sign a waiver if I ever wanted to use the photos but I couldn't resist taking them. I didn't use any flash, just in case. The sound of the shutter wasn't very loud and he stayed asleep. I figured I should let him sleep. He wasn't doing any harm.

As I stood from picking up the watering can, he jerked. Slowly, his arm lifted from his head and he blinked as he looked up at me. His eyes were jade. Iridescently dark then light, almost living colour. For a moment he looked confused then his features tightened in a grimace as he slowly pulled into a sitting position. He had dark hair, not brown exactly. If I had to place a name, I'd call it mahogany. He was vaguely familiar like someone I'd seen long ago, but couldn't quite place, yet at the same time I'd never seen anyone put together quite so perfectly.

It was hard to guess his age. He looked youngish, my age possibly, but he moved like someone older. It was only as his eyes closed and he seemed to be steading himself that I saw the tell-tale signs and caught my breath. He reminded me so much of Aiden. Chalky skin, sallow face, slow movements. The only difference was this guy seemed to still have the muscle mass Aiden had lost. For the first time in years I felt myself choke up at the memories. Swallowing hard, I tried to play it cool. Be normal. Aiden had hated being treated like an invalid even when he'd been forced into a wheelchair. All he wanted was to be treated like normal. I figured this guy would be no different than my brother in that regard.

"Thank you." The guy looked up at me and I nodded at the two empty drink bottles under the seat. "For watering my plants."

"They looked thirsty."

That quirked my amusement and I smiled. Placing the watering can on the ground, I sat at the table with my camera in front of me.

"Am I trespassing?" His voice was low and slightly breathless as he glanced up at me.

"Nope. Not if you're into gardening." I held out my hand. "I'm Nova by the way."

He'd closed his eyes again momentarily so I let my arm drop.

"Nova, it means new."

"Hey, yeah you're right. Most people think it has something to do with the stars. And you are…?"

"Benaiah."

"That's not a name you hear often."

"Neither is Nova."

"Touché. Well, Benaiah, welcome to my sanctuary."

He smiled softly and my heart literally skipped a beat. It was the strangest feeling.

"Some people call me Ben. You're a photographer?"

"Yes." I didn't like the long pause after my answer. "I've been playing around with cameras since I was four. The photos I took with Dad's camera he entered into a show. There wasn't a category for entrants under five years old, so he entered the same photo in the under tens, young artists and candid capture categories and I took out all three first places."

"With the same photo?"

"Yep. He bought me my own camera when I was eight and I've been earning money with it since I was eleven."

"Really?"

"Wonders of the internet."

"Some days you really do meet the most interesting people."

"May I take your photo?"

The expected frown creased his features. People were always so surprised that I wanted to take their photo.

"Why would you want to do that?"

"You're the only thing new in the vista at the moment."

He gave that ghost smile of his, and my heart did its stop-start routine. Heck, I would be in trouble if he decided to ever grace me with an actual smile.

"Sure, whatever."

I took a few extra shots. He didn't look up at me which was great. I loved natural appearing poses over cheesy-grinned portraits any day of the week.

"So…do you live in the building?"

"At the moment."

"Which unit?"

"Are you always this nosy?"

"Yep. Yet somehow I've never been interested in photojournalism. Funny that."

"Seven-Thirty."

I brought the camera down to stare at him. My flat was 731.

"That's why you look vaguely familiar. You're related to the new guy. Zeph Angelis."

Benaiah gave a nod. "Brother."

I tried to show no reaction. If this was the brother, then maybe he had super powers, too. At the moment though, he looked like he'd gone three rounds with Kryptonite.

"Benny?"

We both looked around as the roof door slammed.

"Don't call me that." Benaiah called out.

"You scared the hell out of me, man. I got home and you were…" Zeph came around the corner and came up short as he saw me.

"Getting some air." Benaiah shrugged. "And meeting new people."

"Hi." Zeph greeted. "Zephyris Angelis. Most people call me Zeph."

"I know. Nova Quinn." I thought I sounded fairly calm and collected, considering I was shaking Superman's hand.

"Ah, the elusive flat-mate of Kate and Clancy across the hall."

"Yep. Speaking of elusive, we've been trying to invite you around for dinner one time. Benaiah, you too. Kind of a welcome to the building thing."

I was looking at Zeph but from the corner of my eye, I saw the slight headshake Benaiah gave.

"Thanks, but not right now." Zeph smiled. "Maybe some other time."

I shrugged. "That's cool. It's an open invitation, just let one of us know."

Disappointment rose, mixed with relief as I watched the brothers leave. I didn't take Benaiah's negative response personally. Aiden used to have good days and bad days, and even the good days knocked him around. I was really going to have to brush up on my Superman trivia. Somewhere along the line there had to be a conversation starter on how someone had confronted Clark with the revelation they knew he was Superman. I needed all the help I could get.

Shaking my head at myself, I went back inside. Halting outside the roof door, I overheard them talking.

"You think she's cute." Benaiah laughed.

"Shut it down."

"Well, you do have a thing for brunettes."

"Shut it all the way down."

"You should ask her out."

"Don't make me kill you, *Benny*."

Laughing softly as the door to their unit closed behind them, I couldn't help feeling flattered. One thing was for certain, super powers or not, brothers would be brothers the world over.

Chapter Four

Wincing, I shifted my foot. I had been crouching so long it had gone to sleep. Apart from the roof, one of my favourite haunts was the park as twilight approached. The rush of walkers, joggers and people making their way home from work was starting to ease. There would be more, later, but the sunset was now at the point where I'd lost usable light.

"Can we go now?"

"Yes, Kate. We can go."

Moving from my crouch, I packed up my camera bag as Kate jumped up from one of the tables.

"About time. Feccello's here we come."

Feccello's made the best ice cream and I knew I had just enough cash for a double scoop, so I wasn't about to complain about Kate's impromptu planning. As we walked, she pushed against my shoulder.

"So, you haven't told me what the brother is like."

I shrugged. "I don't know him well enough."

That received an eye roll. "What's he look like?"

"Like Zeph, except green eyes, slightly shorter and I'd have to say more muscular."

"More muscular? Nova, Zeph is buff-osaurus. How can someone be more muscular than that?"

"Different build. Compare a swimmer to a wrestler with a high IQ. I also think he's sick."

"Like, *fully sick*." Kate adopted a 'yo-dude' attitude and did the jab thing with her hands. I'd never been able to understand the meaning behind all that.

"No, I mean like Aiden sick."

Kate stopped dead in her tracks and stared at me with her mouth open. "He's got cancer?"

"I don't know, but there's something."

"Ouch. Bummer."

"Yeah." I needed to change the subject before it became depressing. "What were you doing in the park?"

"Hmm, walking through it. It's a free country."

"Uh-huh."

"Okay, fine. There was a really cute guy that came to work today. My God, Nova, his smile could melt a wicked witch." She fanned herself theatrically with her hand. "I overheard him say he was going to catch up with some friends at Feccello's, and I had a sudden urge for some ice cream. Then I saw you and decided I could do with a wing-man."

It was my turn for the eye-roll. "I thought you had Zeph in your sights."

"We're not dating or anything so any port in a storm."

"What makes you think I want to be your wing-man?"

"Because you've got your camera and Feccello's offers the perfect view down to the Arts Centre and the river."

I laughed. "You really do know how to bribe a girl."

"Yep."

Feccello's wasn't overly crowded but it was decidedly busy. Kate's 'cute guy' was in line for service, so she quickly confirmed I wanted my usual then made a bee-line for the queue. Weaving around occupied tables, I snaffled an empty one and set up my camera for a couple of shots.

"Hi. Are you a photographer?"

I glanced away from the display of my camera, to the guy at the next table. He looked early to mid-twenties and had that superior confident air which screamed 'money'. He sat with a second guy and a girl bearing the same quality and they were all looking at me.

"Yes." I smiled.

"I'm Edward, this is Julius and Viola.

With names like that, they were old money.

"Nova." I reached across to shake the hand he offered. A stabbing pain fired through my hand and I jerked it away. Looking down at it, I couldn't see anything.

"Sorry." I apologised at his curious expression. I gave him the only plausible explanation I could think of. "Static electricity."

"Is it a hobby?" Viola asked. "Your photography?"

"No." I reached into my camera case and handed over a card. "Nova Q Photography."

"You make a living with this?" At least she sounded curious and not rude.

"So the tax man tells me." I smiled.

"Good on you." Edward flicked the card in his fingers. "Do you mind if I keep this?"

"Go ahead. Do you mind if I take your photo?"

I couldn't believe I'd asked. I hadn't planned on it. His smile was slow as if he thought the query had more personal connotations. "Go ahead."

I urged them all into the shot and took a few. Julius crossed to my table to look at the display on my camera. I shivered in the suddenly cool breeze. The evening had been mild until then, but I saw Julius wore gloves.

"May we have copies?"

"If you sign a waiver allowing me to use the photos as marketing if I need to then I can do that."

"Do you happen to have the paperwork?"

Reaching into my bag, I took out the folder.

Edward laughed. "Why am I not surprised?"

They filled in their details and I promised to be in contact within the next few days.

"Ready to go?"

Kate's 'cute guy' had appeared next to their table.

"Sure." They stood and collected their paraphernalia from the backs of their chairs.

Edward leaned across to me again with his hand outstretched. "Nice to meet you, Nova."

"Yeah, likewise."

Gingerly, I took his hand but this time all I felt was the warmth of his grip.

Kate plonked herself down beside me and we watched them leave.

"Check this out." She sang at me as she waved a scrap of paper. "I got his number. Jan Klein. Spelt with a 'J', said with 'Y'."

"Good for you. Which one's mine?" I indicated the desserts melting on the table.

"That one. So, I saw you guys talking." Kate turned her spoon upside down and sucked the ice cream from it. "Did you get a date?"

I laughed as I took a spoonful of my coffee and banana flavoured scoops. "No, but I took a few photos."

"There will be a day, I swear, where you will get your head out from behind that thing and start living."

"I am living."

"Uh-huh. Remind me again, what did you do for your eighteenth birthday?"

"Lots of people work on their birthdays."

"Yep, and how many do it at a shipping yard taking photos of a ship being constructed?"

"It was actually interesting."

"Again, you have to get a life. Maybe I'll have a double date with Jan and you hook up with that guy who was checking you out."

"No one was checking me out."

"Yeah-heah he was. The guy who shook your hand."

"Edward?"

"His name was Edward? Did he sparkle?"

I groaned. "I don't think he was a vampire, besides, if he was, he'd be taken."

"Pity."

"Can we talk about something else please? Something that matters."

"How to get a date 101."

"Must I remind you that the four times you've set me up have not exactly turned out well?"

Kate shrugged. "They can't all be gems. Sometimes you get…that other stuff. What's it called? You know the stuff you scrape off the top."

"Dross?"

"That's it."

Frowning, I heard the scrape of my spoon on the cardboard bottom of the serving bucket. Surely I hadn't finished my ice cream already? Apparently I had.

My mouth felt tacky, like I'd swallowed PVA glue.

"Where are you going?"

"Look after my camera, I'm getting a drink."

"Here, I've got water." Kate rummaged through her bag and pulled out her signature pink water bottle.

Popping the top, I guzzled. My tummy was filling and I paused for breath but my mouth still felt tacky. I'd never had this reaction to ice cream before.

"Whoa, steady on. That's like a litre of water. Actually, you're looking a little flushed. Are you okay?"

"I think there was something wrong with that ice cream."

Kate's hand felt ice cold on my cheek before she quickly moved it to my forehead. "Geez, Nova, you're burning up. Let's get you home."

Grabbing the back of my chair as I stood, it took a moment for the world to stop spinning. I'd never felt quite like this before. Kate wrapped my arm around her shoulder and steadied me with an arm around my

waist. It felt like my body and I weren't quite
connected. Time snapped like a rubber band,
bouncing between fast forward and a stepping pause.
It was far too hot. Within moments, I was soaked with
sweat and I couldn't understand why Kate wouldn't
let me strip off to cool down. She bundled me into the
tram and sat me next to the window. For some reason,
the tram driver had the radio tuned to some station
playing an operatic aria, but he had the volume so
loud I was surprised no one else was complaining.

"Should we ask the driver to turn the music
down?"

"What music?"

I waved a finger around. "The opera."

"Nova…there's no music."

I put my hands over my ears but it didn't stop the
sound. The guy in front of us was playing with an
eReader and abruptly turned.

"Do you really think no one knows?"

"Knows what?"

"Sorry?" Kate leaned in towards me.

I pointed at the guy but he was back to reading his
eReader as though nothing happened.

"Didn't he ask a question?"

"No. I don't like this. Are you going to be okay?"

I couldn't form an answer. It didn't seem that
important. I looked down at the trails of ants under
the window. There had to be nine or ten lines, all
marching ever onwards. I'd never seen so many ants
on a tram before. I peered at the sky. It was clear.
Rain was the only reason I knew for a sudden influx
of insects. No such luck. Obviously, the critters
simply wanted a free ride. Leaning my head against

the glass, I peered outside. Strangely, all the pedestrians were watching the tram. It was really freaky. They had stopped walking and were turned to watch the tram rattle its way down the street. Maybe they didn't like the choice of opera which was blasting at them through the windows. One moment, I watched the Rialto Towers pass the window and the next, Kate was standing to push the red button on the post near the ticket machine. Somewhere I'd lost almost half an hour. I breathed a sigh of relief when I stepped onto the footpath and the opera snapped off as if the driver had finally had enough of that same damn aria.

I tried to take a step toward the front of the building and watched in horror as my feet sank into the cement. If the council was going to work on it, they should have left signs. Kate trekked through the wet cement as if she didn't even notice. She left footprints that filled with red liquid. Frowning, I stared down at it as the metallic scent hit me. Gasping, I screwed my eyes shut. When I opened them, Kate had her arm around my waist as the elevator doors closed.

"Did you see the blood?" I asked as the hum of the elevator vibrated through me.

"What blood?"

"In your footsteps, with the wet cement."

"What the hell are you talking about? This is getting beyond a joke. As soon as we're in the flat, I'm calling an ambulance. Something is seriously wrong with you."

The elevator doors opened and Zeph was standing there. My mouth dropped opened as I stared at him.

"You've got wings."

They were huge. They arched up beyond his head and draped down beside him a good thirty centimetres wider than his arms. There was no way he would have been able to fit them into the elevator.

Beside me, Kate shook her head. "She's hallucinating. I'm calling an ambulance."

"How long has she been doing that?"

His voice was playing at a speed far too slow for the sound. Growling and muffled. Those two words together were so funny. Growling and muffled. It was like a dryer with a tilt. The elevator was quiet and I saw the ants from the tram had hitched a ride in the elevator, too.

"Whoa."

Without warning I was in Zeph's arms. His body and arms were cold through my jeans and the back of my shirt, but I could feel the heat from his wings on my arm and hand as I wrapped it around his neck. The wings were white, but not white. More like staring at black then blinking. I tried to touch them. They were feathered, light and heat, so pretty, but not solid. He wasn't Superman. He was an Angel.

"Angelis. I should have guessed." I laughed.

"Should I call an ambulance?" Kate's voice was suddenly so loud.

"Let Benaiah check her over first. He's studied medicine."

I was on the couch. It wasn't my couch. I could hear faint voices behind me then Benaiah was kneeling. I hadn't even seen him approach.

"Wow, that's so beautiful." I breathed.

He was surrounded by an aura of light. That was
the best I could describe it. It was transparent but
rippling with a rainbow of colours and not more than
5mm thick all the way around him. He placed his
hand on mine and I was fascinated by the way the
aura moved. The swirling colours seemed to sink
from his hand into my skin. It was like being inside a
rainbow. I could feel his other hand on my face, then
pressing into my wrist.

"She's running a temperature and her pulse is fast.
Kate there's a BP cuff in the bathroom. Could you
grab it?"

"A what?"

"Blood pressure. It'll say it on the box."

I looked up at Zeph as he leaned over the back of
the sofa. The light from his wings nearly blinded me.
I looked away to the rainbows sinking into my skin. It
was easier to watch.

"She saw wings."

I pointed up without looking away from the
rainbows. "Sees."

Benaiah's lips compressed as furrows appeared
between his brows. It was fascinating that he could
look so serious and perplexed, and still look so good.

"Fighting…something foreign. I can't…pinpoint. I
don't think I'm strong enough."

"If it was anything else, you know I wouldn't ask."
Zeph told him.

Nodding, Benaiah's grip on my hand tightened.
"Keep her occupied."

Zeph disappeared and I heard his voice asking
what I'd had to eat or drink. His voice faded as a
burst of coloured rain engulfed both Benaiah and me.

Chapter Five

I had a massive headache and felt
discombobulated. Flashes of the strangest dreams
remained in my mind like the scent of smoke. There
was nothing I could quite latch onto. I frowned.
Somehow, I'd ended up in my own bed and I couldn't
track how I got here.

"Hey, how do you feel?"

Squinting, I looked up at Kate. She was a
silhouette in the doorway.

I groaned as I placed the crook of my arm over my
face. "Like I've been hit by a tonne of bricks. Did we
go drinking last night?"

There was a shuffle on the carpet and I could smell
coffee as she came closer. She never brought me
coffee in bed.

"Benaiah seems to think you were slipped a
micky."

I shook my head under my arm. The mention of
his name brought forth a flash of rainbow. "I don't…"

"Someone drugged you. I think it was in the ice
cream."

"Who would…?" I lifted my arm and blinked. Holding my eyes open flared the headache so I stopped trying and dropped my arm back into place.

"I don't know. I've been trying to remember but I don't recall anyone going near enough to the ice cream to do it. I really can't."

Kate's voice held a tremble I recognised. She was on the cusp of blaming herself.

I remembered Kate holding me as we walked away from Feccello's…opera, ants…wings…everything was hazy. My stomach clenched at the idea I'd been drugged, but Kate needed reassuring. "Well, because of you, nothing happened and I'm fine."

"I was going to ring an ambulance but Benaiah looked you over and said you were nearly past the worst of it. He checked on you every hour or so. You didn't get worse and about two hours after we got home it started to wear off. I've never been so relieved. He said you were to stay home today and drink lots and lots of water. Flush it out of your system."

"Is he a doctor?"

"He's studying to be one."

"So I was diagnosed by someone only studying to be a doctor?"

"Well, even the best are just 'practicing physicians'."

I snorted. "Except now I get to suffer a hangover without enjoying the initial stage of the process."

"Sounds about right." Hearing the dull thud on my bedside table I guessed Kate had found a place for the coffee mug. "At least you don't have to deal with Clancy's music this morning."

Listening, I noticed the unusual silence. "Where is he?"

"He picked Joanna up last night. Remember they were going to spend the night at the airport hotel. Privacy."

"Okay. Can I go back to sleep now?"

"Yes, right after you drink this."

It would be too cruel to let her know the last thing I felt like at the moment was the coffee. I cracked an eye open and saw she was holding out a 600ml bottle of water.

"If I drink that I won't get much sleep. I'll be up before long with nature calling."

"Good, then you get to drink another one. Lots of fluids, remember?"

With a groan, I held out my hand and felt the weight of the bottle unceremoniously dumped into it. Kate had the morning off, which meant she would be home to play nursemaid. It was going to be a long day.

By lunch time, I'd had a few hours of extra sleep, eaten, and drunk nearly two litres of water. Except for the annoyance of the regular trips to the bathroom, I felt much better.

"Nova?"

"Hmm?" I acknowledged Kate but didn't turn from the computer screen. I'd had to turn the monitor brightness down to nearly black and I still had my headache. Perhaps it wasn't the best move in the world, but I didn't do idle very well.

"What are you doing?"

"Working on –."

"Stop right there. No work remember?"

"I'm doing a few touch ups. It's not work; it's fun."

"You need to find a better definition of fun. Besides, you should be sleeping, resting and getting better."

"I feel fine and it's not as if I'm running around." I wanted her to go away. I was trying to remove the bright orange wall behind a sleek black spider monkey. Obviously they had modern designers for the zoo enclosures. There was no other way to explain a bright orange wall in an animal habitat. It was such a bad choice.

I hadn't realised Kate had crossed the room until she yanked the scribe from my hand and replaced it with a thick book. I looked down at the clutching half-naked couple on the cover.

"'To Tame a Rake'. What the heck is this?"

"Light reading. Nothing strenuous."

"You really do want me to sleep don't you?"

"It's not that bad. And you don't get this back until tomorrow."

In the reflection of the monitor I saw her waggle the scribe tool.

"Fine." Using the keyboard was clunky but workable. Without warning the monitor went black, plunging the room into darkness. Frowning, I glanced over my shoulder to Kate. There was enough light to see her at the power points casually holding an unplugged cable in her hand. "Come on, Kate, don't be a pain."

She followed the cable around and removed it from my monitor. "I'm holding these for ransom until tomorrow morning at eight o'clock. You can claim them then."

"What am I supposed to do until then?"

"Do you want me to make it eight thirty?"

"Don't you think this is taking things a bit far?"

"You didn't see you last night. So, no I don't think I am. No camera, no photos and no work."

"You're lucky I didn't have any shoots booked for today."

"No, you are. Saved you the hassle of cancelling them."

"You are a pest."

"Takes one to know one." She sang at me as she flicked on the light switch as she left. With a groan, I rested my thumb and finger against my closed eyelids as the headache flared with the invasion of light. She was probably right anyway. The headache wasn't going away despite the painkillers. Truth be told, I think working on the computer had made it worse. With a sigh I trudged through to the lounge room. Normally the darkest room of the flat; with no windows and the only natural light when someone left their bedroom door open, the lounge room was unsurprisingly lit up with every lamp Kate could get her hands on. She loved doing that. Me, I preferred to turn off all the lamps and use the overhead fluoro. I walked around flicking off the collection of lamps then paused with my hand on the light switch. The three bedroom doors were open and so was the one to my studio. The kitchen window was also thrown open. Normally, it gave enough light to navigate without hitting furniture but not enough to read or work on anything with success. Strangely, there was enough light I could still read the silly title of Kate's book. Leaving the light off and dropping onto the couch, I stretched out, staring up at the clichéd cover of her bodice ripper. I could hear the shower running and knew I had some time on my own for at least half an hour. That girl couldn't comprehend the notion of a short shower. With a sigh, I opened the first few pages of the book. I was surprised I could actually read the words. Not that it would have been any great loss if I couldn't. At least this one had a semblance of a story line, and despite the heroine being too independent for a supposed period story it wasn't a bad yarn.

"Kate." I slammed my eyes shut as a soft click turned a flood light on in the room.

"Sorry," Kate apologised. "Were you asleep?"

"I was reading your stupid book." Squinting, I tested the brightness of the light again. It was still a glare.

"You shouldn't read in the dark, you'll ruin your… Oh my God. Nova, your eyes."

I blinked the body part under scrutiny until they adjusted to the light. "What about my eyes? Other than you seem intent on burning the retina out."

"They…they…the whole iris is black."

"What?"

"I'm serious. It's freaky."

"Maybe you're the one who needs sleep."

I gave an exasperated sigh and swung my legs down as she yanked on my arm. She led me to the bathroom, letting go only to wipe the fogged mirror with a towel. I squinted in the bright sunlight and shielded my eyes until they adjusted. My headache flared again with an intensity which made me nauseous.

Kate shoved my shoulders around until I had no choice but to look into the mirror. I could only stare. Normally my eyes were a pale brown, but at the moment they were black; as black as midnight. I couldn't see where my pupil ended and my iris began.

"What the hell?"

"This is so bad. Come on."

I stumbled as Kate pulled at my arm again. "Where are we going?"

"Next door. Maybe Zeph and his brother know what to do. I've never heard of anything like this happening to anyone."

I let her pull me through our flat. I wasn't feeling well and I was more than a little freaked out by now. My eyes were black. That sort of thing only happened in horror movies or TV series about supernatural stuff. I wasn't sure if the Angelis brothers could help me, but a trip across the hallway was better than staring in shock at my reflection. The moment Kate opened our front door and let in the strong sunlight flooding from the large window at the end of the hallway; my headache flared into overdrive. It was as if someone had turned a floodlight in my direction, and it was burning into my head. Dropping to the floor, I screwed my eyes shut and covered them with my hands.

"Nova?"

"Light hurts." I managed around clenched teeth.

Kate muttered. "Not surprised."

I heard her pounding on the door across the way. I expected the sound to flare the headache like the time

I had a migraine, but it didn't. With my eyes shut and covered and my back to the light the headache stabilized to a bearable agony. I was contemplating feeling my way back inside our unit when I felt a masculine hand on my shoulder. Warmth radiated and within moments the headache was gone as if it had never been.

"Nova? Can you open your eyes for me?"

I didn't move at the sound of Benaiah's voice. "There's too much light."

The sound of movement came and a new scent wafted. I realised that Benaiah smelt softly woody; as if he'd spent the day working with timber and had only recently been covered in sawdust. The new scent was more like warm salt air faintly on a breeze.

"Can you make it back to your apartment?" Zeph asked.

"Why?" Benaiah asked softly.

"We're making a scene in the hallway." Zeph answered just as softly.

That was encouragement enough for me. I liked to be behind the scenes, not creating them. Using the wall and the touch on my shoulder as a guide, I made my way back inside and dropped on the couch.

The low light of the lamp was as bright as the fluoro overhead usually was, but not unbearable. What made me close my eyes and open them a few times was something else entirely. Obviously, I wasn't dreaming last night. Or I was dreaming now. Benaiah was surrounded by a rainbow glow and Zeph sported his larger than life angel wings. I slid a look over to Kate. She looked worried and was chewing a thumbnail, but she wasn't reacting to their… additions. In fact, as she paced she passed directly through Zeph's wings. I blinked as a bright light came near my face. Benaiah was holding a small torch. He acted like he was testing the dilation of my eyes except he never actually shone the light into them. For which I was grateful. His rainbow glow was sliding from his hand on my shoulder and under my skin. It was weird and pretty. It should have been freaking me out but it wasn't.

"That's impossible," Zeph said from behind Benaiah.

"The foreign body is gone. I can't find anything."

"I've only seen eyes like that on children."

"And there is nothing physically wrong."

My heart pounded. Benaiah's mouth had stayed shut during that exchange. And Kate didn't react. She was standing directly next to Zeph. She would definitely have commented on the 'children' remark. Rainbow glows and angel wings no one else could see. Mind talking…or whatever that was. Then there were my freaky eyes. A girl could only take so much.

"Would you mind telling me what is going on?"

"Probably a delayed reaction to the drugs." This time Benaiah's mouth moved.

"That's bull and you know it."

"Nova, take it easy. They're trying to help."

I ignored Kate. "Okay, Mr Angelis…" I glared at Benaiah. "How much is medical knowledge and how much is rainbow magic?"

He frowned but Kate got in first. "Are you upset he hasn't finished his degree? Without him, I wouldn't have known what to do last night…"

I continued to ignore Kate's effort to placate me. Concentrating on the two brothers, I figured if I could hear them, they might be able to hear me. I didn't really think it through. I wanted to cut through the crap.

"And what the hell do you mean about the children with eyes like this?"

As I thought the words I realised they felt weird. Normally thoughts wander around your head as easily as a spoken word. This one felt like it was moving through fridge chilled honey. It certainly got their attention.

"That's impossible."

I glared at Zeph. *"Stop saying that. Obviously it's not."*

"It is, however, unexpected." Benaiah calmly hooked the small torch onto his keys. *"Certainly we need to talk about this but not in front of Kate. It'll be odd if we continue to glare at each other in silence."*

"Your proposition?" Zeph didn't move, but I could almost hear crossed arms in his thought.

"We'll meet on the roof at seven. The sun will have gone down by then and we can talk."

"And that'll give you enough time to have a 'what the hell' session back at your place, and come up with some answers."

Benaiah gave a little half smile at my comment. *"Something like that."*

"Fine." I uncrossed my arms as I scrambled to think back to where we were in the actually spoken conversation. "So your diagnosis, Dr Angelis?"

"You're eyes are over dilated and not returning to normal as quickly as they should, giving you sensitivity to light, and causing you pain. Stay in the dark as much as possible and continue resting."

"That's all you've got?"

"That's all I've got."

I snorted and quipped sarcastically. "Take two aspirin and I'll see you in the morning."

Benaiah shrugged. "If it helps with the headache, by all means."

"Smartarse." I muttered, trying not to laugh. As upside down as everything was at the moment, there was something charming about the Angelis brothers. Well, one at any rate. Mr 'It's impossible' was watching me as if I'd stolen the Hope diamond.

Benaiah's half smile came again before he stood and turned to Kate. "She'll be fine."

Chapter Six

I held my camera in my hands but it was a silent prop. My pretence at normality. I'd worn sunnies and watched the sunset. Now the eyewear sat atop my head as I knelt at the balustrade and gazed over the city. It was eerie. Normally, the city lights glinted and glowed giving the view a Christmas tree effect. This time, lights flooded the surrounding areas in pools of shine which hazed outwards, illuminating more than they'd ever done before. I saw the expected shadows of night but it wasn't completely dark. They were exposed in soft greys. It was as if the extraneous glow of lights from the city which normally hid the stars from view was rebounding off the sky and giving extra light to the area. While it wasn't as crisp as daylight, I could see everything. My freaky eyes were giving me almighty night vision.

I smiled as I spotted a couple on the street. He was in dress pants, white shirt and black vest. She was in a slinky, red dress covered by his jacket. They was walking slowly and holding hands. Automatically, I flicked the lens cap off and tucked it into the pocket of my jeans as I brought the camera into position.

After a few frustrating moments I swore as I lowered it again. There was nothing visible through the camera but indistinguishable shadows in the dark. Even then it was only a hint. It didn't give me what I could actually see. It was ridiculous.

Movement made me look up. For some reason I wasn't surprised as I watched Zeph descend. He wore boots but made no sound as he landed on the roof. He avoided the wash from the security light.

"You want to be careful doing that." I told him.

He stiffened and frowned as his eyes searched. Cocking his head, he held himself still and seemed to wait.

"Yes, Zeph, I'm talking to you."

If anything, that seemed to cause him more shock. Slowly, he moved toward me, but it was slow and cautious. He stopped a few feet away, his eyes still searching. It was only then I realised I was hidden in the shadows. He couldn't see me. That amused me.

"Getting warmer." I laughed softly.

"You can see me?"

"Well, duh. I'm not exactly talking to myself here."

"That's impossible."

"It's official. That has to be your favourite phrase."

Zeph rippled. There was no other way to describe it. It was like a watery, wavy, shield had been surrounding him and it rippled into nothing, leaving him more…solid. And suddenly he had a shadow, which until that very moment I hadn't noticed he'd been missing.

"Okay." I said slowly. "What just happened?"

"I became visible."

I shook my head. That didn't make sense. "Sorry. What?"

"Visible. The opposite to invisible. Except to you it would seem."

"Me?"

"Yes. You shouldn't have been able to."

I wasn't the dullest tool in the shed but this conversation made no sense. I kept my mouth shut for a moment trying to sort it out.

"Do you mean to tell me, you can become invisible? And that you were and now you're not."

He made a 'well, duh' gesture. It wasn't quite aimed at my direction, but I caught the gist.

"So…what? I can see you when you are invisible?"

Zeph did the ripple thing again and his shadow disappeared.

"I don't know. You tell me." He challenged.

Without a sound he moved over to the bench and sat. I don't know how he did that without crushing his wings. If anything, they passed through the wood and metal behind him. The bench was flooded from the security light and he still had no shadow. Rising from my knees, I slid my sunnies back over my eyes and sat next to him.

"It would appear so." I went to pat his leg but my hand went through him. "Whoa."

Zeph smiled. "That part is handy when you're trying not be noticed."

It was only then I realised he wasn't talking. At least not with his voice.

"How do you do that? The talking in my head thing?"

He stood. *"Come with me."*

"I thought we were waiting for Benaiah."

"You've just changed the ball game."

I decided silence was the better part of valour and followed him to the door of his unit. My stomach churned though I hadn't been able to eat anything all afternoon. I tried every breathing exercise I'd ever heard of but it didn't ease the sense of impending calamity. Normal life didn't have all the strangeness which had entered my life within the last twenty-four hours. And it had been only twenty-four hours. Nearly. Give or take.

Zeph unlocked his door and indicated I should go first. The layout of the unit was the exact mirror of ours but that was where the similarities ended. Their place was so sparse in furniture it looked almost sterile. What it lacked in furnishings it made up in computers, cables and impressive looking technological stuff.

"Do you guys work for the FBI or something?"

"Nova?" Benaiah was hidden behind a row of screens and he scattered papers as he stood. "Is it seven already? Zeph isn't back yet. How did you get in here?"

Blinking, I glanced between the two brothers. Zeph was standing in the middle of the…I looked at the floor. No shadow.

"This can't be for real. You really can't see him? This isn't some sort of game?"

"Zeph?"

"I'm here."

Benaiah glanced around the room then snapped his attention to me. "Wait, you can see him?"

"He's standing right there."

He pulled his ripple thing then went to collect the papers Benaiah had scattered. Benaiah for his part was staring at me as if I'd grown an extra head. I suppose watching his brother ripple in from mid-air was something he'd grown up seeing. Or not seeing.

"What?" I shifted uncomfortably at the intensity of his stare. "And don't say it's impossible because that's his line."

Benaiah turned to Zeph. "Where's Ransom?"

"He's coming. He doesn't like to fly."

"Who's Ransom?"

"A friend." Benaiah glanced back at me.

"Do you all have strange names? And can I sit down?"

Zeph handed the papers to his brother and emptied a chair of its collection of boxes. "Want a coffee too?"

"I'm good. I've had so much water today I'm sloshing." I sat on the chair and placed my camera on an unclaimed spare inch or three of the table. It was the only clear space it had. "So is someone going to tell me what the hell is going on?"

"How are your eyes?" Benaiah asked. It felt like he was avoiding my question.

"Fine as long as I keep the sunnies on."

"May I see?"

"Why? Are you going to pull more rainbow magic?"

His brow creased. "Rainbow magic?"

"Your rainbow…aura…thing. When you touch me
it disappears into my skin. I mean it's pretty and all
but…" Benaiah's frown deepened as he looked down
at himself then back at me with a curious expression.
My stomach clenched and I felt a rise of bile. "You
don't see it, do you? And you don't see Zeph's wings
either. Have I gone mad?"

"No. I think you are seeing."

"Oh yeah. I'm seeing things alright."

Benaiah pulled the office chair around the table as
Zeph arrived with two mugs of coffee and handed one
to his brother. "Not seeing things. Seeing. This is
going to sound stranger than fiction but –."

"When I was eight there was a woman who once told
me I had beautiful wings," Zeph interrupted. "Most
people thought she was mad so didn't pay her any
attention, but I knew she was onto something because
I already knew I could fly. We know you can see me
when I'm invisible and you see the wings. You see
what is there."

"Zeph, you can't just…"

"Cool it, man. She saw me fly and didn't freak out
about it, so you don't need to."

"Oh, I freaked out about it, believe you me. I don't
know what your rainbow means though."

Benaiah took a sip of his brew before he answered.
"When I touch people I heal them."

"But you can't heal yourself?"

Benaiah nodded. "I can."

"But you…well, you look…"

"If I heal too much I wear myself out. That's why I
don't often go out in public. I can't pick and choose
who I'm going to heal. The instant I touch skin to

skin, it happens. I can heal my body, but it takes time for the weariness to dissipate."

I could see he already looked healthier than he had a couple of weeks ago, and even in a day his aura had grown a little thicker. It made sense.

"That's why it goes into my skin when you touch me. You use it to heal but it takes time for your aura to regenerate."

"Maybe that's how it works, I don't know."

"You don't know how it works?"

Benaiah ran a hand through his hair making it more rumpled than it already was but it was Zeph who answered.

"It's like your heartbeat. Granted there are some people who have strength of mind to consciously make it beat faster or slower, but for most people it beats without conscious effort. It speeds up when you're active and slows when you're resting. You don't think about it, it simply happens. Like Benny's healing and my flying or my invisibility."

"Don't call me that." Benaiah muttered. "And how did you get so smart anyway?"

"I learned a few things while you were…away."

Obviously Zeph changed the end of his sentence at Benaiah's sharp intake of breath, but the information didn't make things clearer.

"Are you aliens?"

The brothers laughed.

"No, not aliens." Benaiah smiled. "At least not little green men."

I was right about one thing. His full smile was stunning. I near on melted to mush. It was disappointing to watch it slowly fade. I couldn't believe I was reacting to it at this point in time but I couldn't help it.

"We are, however, descendants of Angels."

Zeph's words caught my attention and I stared at him. "Angels?"

"We're Nephilim."

I blinked, not sure I'd heard correctly. "Nephilim? As in 'the mighty men who were of old, the men of renown'?"

"Ah, you've heard of us." Zeph winked.

"I do read my Bible, but you're having me on, right?"

"Sorry to disappoint you." Zeph seemed to think it was all some great joke.

At least Benaiah appeared sombre and somewhat concerned. "Do you need a minute?"

Slumping back in my chair, I held a hand to my suddenly churning stomach and stared between the brothers. If I discounted the fact I could see wings and rainbows, I'd seen one brother fly and heard the other profess to the ability of instant healing.

Nephilim.

An easily missed paragraph in Genesis announcing the name of the breed between Angels and daughters of men; and they were sitting right in front of me.

"Excuse me."

I was glad I knew the layout of their unit because I almost didn't make it to the bathroom in time. The heaving continued even after I'd emptied my stomach of its contents. My stomach hurt, so did my chest, throat, ears, head and I was crying. I always did after throwing up. I wanted to go back to yesterday when life was normal. This bombshell was logical and it scared the hell out of me. I believed what the Bible said about God and Jesus, so therefore I had to believe the existence of Nephilim was plausible. That much I could get my head around. Having them as neighbours was something else entirely. People with Angel type superpowers only existed in movies and books. Yet, here they were.

Exhausted, I leaned against the wall. I felt a hand take mine and within moments the dizziness subsided along with all the painful effects of being sick. The exhaustion dissipated as well, so did the nagging pain in my abdomen which was announcing the arrival of my period in less than forty-eight hours.

"Are you alright?"

"You know I am." I muttered without moving. "You just healed me."

"I can heal physical ailments, not emotional ones," Benaiah said softly. "And there's a new toothbrush under the sink you can use."

Groaning, I covered my face with my hands as he moved away. Just what I needed right then. A reminder that I was never a pretty sight after being sick and that my breath was horrendous.

I took up his offer and brushed my teeth. My reflection showed that I looked normal. No blotchy cheeks, no pale skin. I wasn't game to take off the sunnies under the bright light but I was willing to bet no puffy and red eyes either. Having Benaiah around sure had its benefits.

Back in the lounge room, Zeph still straddled the chair with his drink in his hand. Benaiah leaned back against the table, his hands resting on the surface, and his long legs crossed in front of him. Both of them turned to me as I crossed the threshold.

"That was eventful." Zeph quipped. "Are you done with being dramatic?"

Benaiah glared at him but I gave a small smile. "I haven't even started."

Zeph gave a nod and returned the smile. "That a girl."

"So…" I said slowly as I approached Zeph and held my hand out to his wings. They were amazingly intricate in detail. I could see each strand of feather as they fed the high arch above his shoulders and trailed behind him on the floor. I could feel warmth as my hand passed through them. "…You're Nephilim. Are there more of you?"

"Many. Each generation has less and less Angel blood running through their veins. There are some of us out there with so much human blood that they have no abilities."

"But not you."

Zeph's grin came again. "But not us."

"Flying, invisibility and healing. What other abilities are there?"

"As numerous as the stars. No two Nephilim have the same abilities."

"If they have the same result they don't have the same application." Benaiah added.

"So how come we haven't heard of you? Mainstream I mean, not just those of us who read Genesis."

"So you've never read Ancient Greek myths? Heard of their so called gods?"

I blinked at Zeph as a few names came to mind. "Are you saying the Greek gods were Nephilim?"

"Some of them were Angels, most of the Titans you've read about were Nephilim."

"Hercules?"

"Nephilim."

"Zeus?"

"Angel."

"Aphrodite?"

"Nephilim."

"Athena?"

"Angel. I think."

I retook my seat and cocked my head at Zeph. "You think?"

"When you've been around a while you forget things, and I was never well read on the topic anyway."

"So who are you related to? Icarus?"

"Very funny." Zeph said dryly. "I can tell you who our grandfather was and who my father is but I'm not all that fussed about family trees."

I turned to Benaiah. "What about you? Do you know which Greek god the two of you are related to?"

Benaiah glanced down at the floor as he pushed away from the table. "It's far too complicated.

I wasn't sure if that was an answer or an avoidance. Before I could ask, a knock came at the door.

"About time." Zeph muttered as his brother headed for the door.

Benaiah admitted the biggest, blackest man I have ever seen. He was even taller than Zeph, though not as tall as the tops of Zeph's wings but nearly as wide, and pure ebony. For a moment, I wasn't sure he wore a shirt until he moved to shake Zeph's hand and I saw the shape of the long sleeves and the neckline. It was as black as he was. Thankfully, he wore jeans and not black pants. What held my attention was not his size or skin colour but the golden tattoos which ran in irregular lines over the backs of his hands and his knuckles. The tattoos also covered parts of his neck and face. I wasn't sure what it was supposed to symbolise but it was impressive.

"Nova, this is Ransom. Ransom this is Nova, our neighbour."

Automatically, I stood. I felt utterly dwarfed sitting down, but standing didn't help much. At five-eight, my eyes drew level with the top of his abdomen. I swear, I had to look up another two feet to see his face. Alright, maybe that was a slight exaggeration, but only slight.

He gave a nod and swallowed my hand in a handshake. As his hand flexed, parts of the tattoos moved. They disappeared and reappeared again. I stared as he dropped his hand, just to make sure I wasn't seeing things.

"Ease theese da wane?"

Even in mind speak he had an accent as thick as molasses. It took me a moment to figure out what he'd actually asked.

"Yes." Zeph answered him while Benaiah nodded.

"The one what?" I frowned.

"Da wane whoo tubby dusted."

Taking a step back I nearly lost my balance as I collided with my chair but managed to stay upright. "What sort of test? For what?"

"Tarcee eff ewwbee na far limb."

Ransom's voiced accent was just as thick and so low, the sound vibrated through me.

"Hell no. I'm not a Nephilim. I can tell you that without any testing."

Zeph arched his eyebrows. *"Only Nephilim can Apath."*

Chapter Seven

The room spun as I stumbled the inches to the chair.

"Bathroom's that way." Zeph pointed helpfully.

"There's nothing left." I muttered absently.

There was no need to clarify. It was fairly obvious that 'Apath' was the name for the mind speak thing they did.

That I did.

"I don't understand. I'm human." I looked up at all of them. I was already overwhelmed but having three tall men surrounding me didn't help. "Could you all sit down or move away or something?"

In almost choreographed movements, they all sat. Benaiah sat in his chair, Zeph straddled his and Ransom sank cross-legged onto the floor next to me.

"As best I can figure…" Benaiah leant forward with his hands clasped loosely between his knees. "…twenty-four hours ago you were human, but something happened last night which changed that."

"Despite what Kate seems to think, it wasn't your ice cream." Zeph added.

"Nothing you ingested could have possibly had this effect. When I healed you last night there was something foreign in your blood. Your hallucinations were the side effect of your body fighting the invasion."

I shook my head. "Not drugs."

"I don't think so. This afternoon the foreign body was gone, but you can now Apath and see certain images which I think are some sort of reflection of our Nephilim abilities. This has never happened before but I think by healing you, I may have actually cemented the change."

Zeph placed his chin on his fist against the back of the chair. "We asked Ransom here to positively identify if our theory is correct or if something else is going on."

"The theory that I am now Nephilim?"

"That would be the one." Zeph shrugged.

"And if you're wrong?"

"Then it's a whole 'nother ball game."

I wondered if everything was a joke to him. Perhaps he was attempting to keep the mood light but it really wasn't appreciated right now.

Swallowing hard, I had to ask the obvious question. "And if you're right?"

"Then our next step is to figure out how it came to be." Benaiah's calm tone was easier to handle than his brother's quips.

"So what's the test?"

"Ransom has the ability to identify Nephilim DNA."

"That's kinda…creepy."

Zeph snorted a laugh. "You ain't seen nothing yet."

Benaiah continued as if he hadn't been interrupted. "How this works is to take blood from you both and mix them. If there is Nephilim DNA in your blood it will turn—"

"Gold?" I guessed.

All three of them shared identical shocked looks and it was my turn to smile.

"I thought he had golden tattoos. It's golden veins."

Ransom looked down at himself with the same confused expression as Benaiah displayed when I told him he wore rainbows.

"It would appear part of your theory is correct," Zeph told his brother. "She can see an image representing our abilities."

"I can see through yours." I scowled. He made me feel like an abstract artwork.

Clearly unperturbed, he shrugged. "True."

"How did you discover that this was your ability?"

Ransom turned his head, his face expressionless. "You do not wish to know."

His accent was still thick but I was starting to understand it better.

"Come on." Zeph lifted off his chair. "Let's get this over with."

I was stunned. "Are you that eager to prove I'm a freak?"

"That would make us freaks too, babe."

"Yeah, but at least you're a freak of nature."

I was glad they laughed because I couldn't believe the words came from my mouth. Ransom grabbed the backpack he'd dropped next to him and pulled out a zippered kit of some sort. I recognised it as soon as he opened it.

"Are you diabetic?"

"Hypoglycaemic."

"How is that not diabetic?"

"My body produces a high base line of insulin."

That surprised me. "So Nephilim can get sick?"

"Asks the one who just barfed."

I glared at Zeph but turned my attention back to Ransom as he continued to speak as if Zeph hadn't interrupted.

"The higher the percentage of human bloodline, the more prone to illness. However the ability to combat illness and disease is far greater when Nephilim genetics is present."

"So you have more human blood than Nephilim?"

"Ancestrally, it is an equal balance."

"And yet you are the flip side of diabetic. How can that be?"

"It is what it is. Your hand please."

A part of me wanted to keep my hands to myself. If I didn't go through this 'testing' I could pretend everything was fine. That life was normal. That my eyes were some sort of, hopefully, temporary side effect of being drugged. Looking down at the gold rivers in the hand Ransom held out, I knew I couldn't bury my head in the sand too much longer. My life had changed whether or not I wanted to pretend otherwise. The sooner the confirmation was out of the way the sooner I could work on something practical to deal with it. I held out my hand and Ransom pressed a device to my finger. A few seconds later a loud clunk sounded and a short, sharp pain hit my flesh. Ransom didn't wait for me to react with more than a gasp before he squeezed a drop of blood from my finger onto what looked like a glass slide from the microscopes in biology class back in high school.

He unscrewed the device, swapped out the nasty looking shunt thing, and repeated the procedure on himself. To my surprise, the blood he squeezed from his finger formed a red drop. It didn't stay that way for long. I was expecting lingering anticipation as we waited like witches around a caldron for the spell to work, but it was sadly anticlimactic. The instant his blood dropped from his finger onto the glass slide, a gold smear appeared.

I couldn't pretend any longer, but by this stage I wasn't really surprised. "So what now?"

"The speed of the change and the hue of gold indicates a strong Nephilim gene. We find which family member of hers is part of our race."

"I don't think it's that simple Ransom." Benaiah was playing with the handle of his coffee mug but at least he wasn't pacing like Zeph. "Two days ago she had no abilities. The oldest child recorded to show abilities was seven."

"Either she's the oldest to ever show abilities or there is something else going on. Although her eyes are like a child's. I wonder if that means something." Zeph kept pacing.

"You have pitch eyes?" Ransom's voice rumbled low as he rose from the floor. For a big man he certainly was graceful.

"If pitch means black. So what's the deal with kids and their eyes anyway?"

"A child born with pitch eyes will have abilities. At a time between two and four months their eyes will become…coloured, as all human eyes are."

"Are they sensitive to light?"

"No more than usual for an infant."

"Well, my eyes kicked in after I saw Zeph's wings and Benaiah's rainbow aura."

Ransom tossed his bag in the corner by the front door. "Yes, perhaps it is time for you to tell what has happened in the hours before this."

I shrugged. "I was taking photos in the park, Kate came by and we went to Feccello's. I had my usual scoops, then I don't actually remember much until I woke up this morning. A few flashes but nothing definitive."

"You were hallucinating when Kate brought you in." Zeph added. "Not only the wings and rainbows which we know weren't hallucinations, but you kept talking about insects and blood."

"And you kept telling us to turn down some crazy opera." Benaiah put his coffee on the table. "Do you still have the photos on your camera? The ones you took last night?"

"Yes." I reached for my camera and automatically hooked the strap over my neck. "I would usually have copied them across to my computer by now, but I couldn't be bothered earlier."

Flicking the camera on, I switched it over to preview mode. I was glad I had the camera secure because I nearly dropped it at the first photo displayed.

"Holy Mother of –."

"She was human and she thought her son was crazy for the most part," Ransom muttered. "Nothing Holy about that."

"What?"

"Ignore him. It's a particular bone he gnaws on." Zeph told me. "What's the photo?"

"I took photos of three rich kids last night and now they've got added extras they didn't have then. Look."

I turned the camera around but kept hold of it with the strap.

Zeph shook his head. "I don't recognise them."

"Me neither." Benaiah shrugged.

"This one I know." Ransom tapped the display. "He is one-eighth Nephilim. His grandfather is Lauder."

Zeph and Benaiah both snorted.

"Is that bad?"

"Lauder's bad news," Zeph said. "Some Nephilim believe humans are polluting the gene pool and their aim is to purify the bloodlines. He's one of them."

"It's not really going their way if Edward is one-eighth."

"Edward?"

"That's what he said his name was."

"I thought you couldn't remember last night." Zeph narrowed his eyes.

"I met them before the ice cream."

"What do you see on them?" Benaiah asked.

I glanced back down at the display. "Viola, the girl, has a red glow at her throat. This guy, Julius, has kind of frost, I think, on his skin and Edward has grey spikes, sort of like porcupine quills." I frowned.

"Spikes? Hang on. When I shook his hand, I thought it was static electricity, but what if it wasn't. What if he jabbed me with something?"

"Injected you with the Nephilim gene? That's a bit far-fetched, even for us." Zeph scoffed.

"For the offspring of Lauder it might not be." Ransom said quietly.

"Seriously, dude? Injecting strange girls with the Nephilim gene then letting them wander back to their lives? He would have snatched her. Nova was out of it and Kate's what, five-three in thick socks? She wouldn't have been able to stop three of them."

"Four. Jan Klein, but I didn't get his photo."

I jerked out of the way as a coffee mug shattered.

"Benaiah?"

Zeph went to his brother as Benaiah disappeared into the kitchen.

"I didn't think it was possible to shatter ceramic like that." I quipped to Ransom. He held out his hand in a gesture for silence as the brothers' voices came through the open doorway.

"Will this never end?"

"You don't know –"

"Jan Klein is here, Zeph. Somehow he's followed me. Do you think it's a coincidence that they happened to get Nova? The only other person I've had contact with since I got here."

"It could be another Jan Klein."

"Who happens to hang around with a group of Nephilim? We have to get out. We have to leave. I have to leave."

"We're so close Benny. We find him and –."

"And what? He's just supposed to fix everything? If Ransom's right they'll strip him of his genes and we might as well be back in the days before Noah. This is never going to end."

"Oh, there's an end." Zeph's voice held a smile. "That much was promised."

I heard a hard exhale of breath and imagined Benaiah running his hand through his hair. "You know what I mean."

"I do. Now, are you finished freaking out? Because we've got to come up with an explanation for this little outburst."

"You handle it. I need…"

Benaiah abruptly left the kitchen and headed to one of the bedrooms, closing the door behind him. Zeph came out of the kitchen and glanced at us.

"He'll be fine, he needs some time."

"So who's Jan Klein when he's at home?"

I wasn't about to ignore what just happened, even if I was sure Zeph would have liked me to. Zeph ran a hand over his face with a sigh.

"He's… Lauder's defence secretary for want of a better comparison."

"He's a personal assistant?"

"No, he's a military advisor. Like if Lauder was President."

Just like a Yank. Assuming the whole world ran to the tune of star-spangled-banner. I shrugged. "American politics. That's where you lost me."

"He's –."

"No, I get it. I've seen enough movies. In short…he's also bad news." Zeph nodded and I tried my luck. "So where does Benaiah fit into the news story?"

"Lauder wants his ability for some secret pet project and didn't take kindly to being told no. We got him out and now it looks like Jan has tracked him here. There's no other explanation as to why he happens to be in this very city and not in the States."

"Like a tracking device or something?"

Zeph shook his head. "It's not in Benny, that's for sure. His body would have rejected it moments after it was in. It'll be a Nephilim."

"I'm not sure I like this 'good-guy-bad-guy' idea," I muttered as I bent down to pick up the pieces of broken mug.

"It is a common trait in humans." Ransom pointed out. "How do you know we are not the 'bad'? Unless you measure against a common guide, it is all down to a point of view."

I was speechless as I slowly stood. It wasn't something I wanted to consider, even if it was morbidly logical. Simply because I'd encountered their side first, did not make them the 'good' side. Dumping the pieces of mug onto the table, I grabbed my camera and left without saying goodbye. Too much, way too much. I needed out.

Chapter Eight

"Last time."

Taking slow breaths, I opened my eyes as a circle of light was placed directly to my right eye. The headache flared and I gritted my teeth, praying this would be over soon. The light finally flicked off.

"Finished now. The good news is you've got twenty-twenty vision." I kept my eyes closed as the optometrist pulled the machinery away from my face. "I'm going to turn on the lamp now so I can see."

I heard the click as I brought my sunnies up from my lap.

"I've never seen anything like this." The optometrist, I think his name was Michael-something-or-other, wheeled back to his desk.

"That's comforting."

"I wouldn't say there's anything wrong with your eyes, but this is amazing. Humans don't have a Tapetum lucidum and I can't see one in your eyes but there is definite eye-shine. It's like a rainbow."

"In English?"

"A Tapetum lucidum is a layer of tissue in the eye behind the retina which reflects visible light back though the retina, increasing the light available to the photoreceptors. It's basically what gives animals their night vision."

"And humans don't have one."

"No, but you're displaying effects of having one."

"Are animals sensitive to light too?"

"I don't think so. But I'd say this does have something to do with your extreme sensitivity to light. This degree of photophobia isn't normally present in eyes as dark as yours. Not impossible mind, just unusual. I'm going to give you a referral to an eye specialist and a neurologist."

"A neurologist? As in brain?"

Michael nodded. "Not all photophobia is eye related and I want to make sure we've covered all the bases."

"Great." I sighed. I felt like a lab rat already and I hadn't even left his office. "And what do I do in the meantime?"

"I would recommend a more suited pair of sunglasses, ones with photochromic and polarised lenses."

"Again in English?"

Michael smiled. "They'll be like a normal pair of sunglasses but will darken further in UV light and the polarisation will help stop glare. If that doesn't help we'll see what the Ophthalmologist finds and perhaps try prosthetic lenses to reduce the amount of light entering your eyes."

"And prosthetic lenses are…?"

"Contact lenses."

"Right. Are we done?"

"Let me print out these referrals and you can be on your way."

It was the first time I had ever spent four hundred dollars on a pair of sunglasses. I hoped they were worth it but it was going to take eight to ten working days to find out. I would get a text message when they arrived. Stepping into the shopping centre from the optometrist I felt someone touch my arm.

"Hey, Nova."

Slowly I turned to face Zeph with a sigh. "What do you want?"

He held up his hands in surrender. "Kate mentioned that you were seeing the optometrist today and Benny wanted to make sure you were okay."

"Kate happened to mention? I didn't realise you two were that close already."

Zeph gave a cocky smile. "We were going up in the elevator together. She is cute you know."

"Whatever."

"Why are you mad at me?"

Tilting my head, I realised I was acting waspish. "Sorry. I've got a constant headache, apparently my eyes are photophobic and they do an amazing eye-shine thing. I can't take photos, I can't edit photos, it's nearly impossible to work at a computer…and I've had a week of being nauseous and in pain because of these stupid eyes. I don't know, I just…want the world to stop."

"Benny could help with some of that."

"No. Healing wears him out. Besides, feeling no pain at all…that could easily become addictive. My life is crazy enough without that."

"So do I go back and report that you're okay…or what?"

I laughed ironically then shook my head. "I don't know if I'll ever be 'okay' again."

"Have you taken painkillers recently?"

"There's a chemist over there. I was going to grab some more."

"Banana and coffee, right?"

"What?"

"Ice cream. You like banana and coffee?"

"Yes?" I said cautiously.

"You go to the drugstore and I'll meet you at the food court. We'll pretend the world has stopped for a moment just to allow us time to enjoy some ice cream."

With that, Zeph walked off as if it had been decided. For a moment I was annoyed at his high handedness then gave up. Being annoyed took too much effort.

At least my last experience hadn't tainted the enjoyment of ice cream. I wasn't going to admit it to him but I loved the idea of just sitting and not worrying about anything for a moment. For someone who seemed so outgoing, it was nice to find that he could simply sit quietly and watch the world pass by. Kate would have been chatting about goodness knows what by now and wanting my input too.

Both of us jumped as my phone rang. It wasn't a number I recognised.

"Nova speaking."

"Nova, hi. It's Edward."

My heart jumped into overdrive and I tapped Zeph on the knee. "Edward?"

"Yes. We met at the ice cream place over a week ago. I wanted to ask about the photos."

"Oh, right. Edward if you give me a moment. I'm in a crowd at the moment, let me find somewhere quieter."

Lowering my voice, I held the phone to my body. "What do I do?"

Zeph looked around and quickly led me down the hallway past the bathrooms to the emergency exit. When we stopped, he made a movement with his hand indicating that I should talk to Edward.

I switched the phone to speaker. "Edward are you still there?"

"Yes."

"Great. The photos, did you want copies?"

"Well, I did want to look at them at least, and perhaps take copies, yes."

Beside me Zeph frowned and slowly nodded.

"Sure, no worries. Have you got a pen?" Suddenly Zeph shook his head. "Hang on Edward, I can't figure out how to access my booking calendar and talk on the phone at the same time. The number you're calling from, can I call you back in a few minutes?"

"Sure."

"Thanks."

Without saying goodbye I hung up on him. It wasn't my most professional move but I wasn't too worried about that at the moment.

"Can you make up your mind?" I hissed at Zeph as he pulled out his phone and dialled.

"I don't want him too close to Benny. Not with Jan waiting in the wings. Your place is no good."

"Can't Benaiah go somewhere else for a few hours?"

"Kate could let the cat out of the bag, and letting him know where you live is not a good idea anyway. Hang on." He tilted his head and spoke into the handset. "Hey, Edward's contacted Nova for the photos. What's the game plan?"

Whatever the answer was, it seemed to take a long time.

"Nova, is there a place you can ask him to meet you? Not the apartments."

I thought about it for a minute. "I hire a studio occasionally. They've got a viewing room for proofs. I'll have to see if it's available."

"She's checking." Zeph told the phone. I could only assume he was talking to Benaiah.

I made the call. "Tomorrow afternoon at three."

Zeph relayed that then nodded. "Book it."

After I hung up the phone with Edward I crossed my arms. "Okay, so are you going to tell me why I just booked an appointment with a Nephilim who infected me? You do realise I'm going to be in a room alone with him."

"I'll be there. We want to track him, find out where he's located. We need to find out how many he's here with."

"The Angelis brothers. A fine army."

Zeph laughed. "You have no idea."

Chapter Nine

"Are you going out?"

I finished tying my scarf. Clancy was eating something from a bowl. Probably cereal. He'd eat cereal all day if he could.

"Yeah, I've got a proof showing at three."

"It's just past midday. Don't you think it's a little early?"

"I've got some stuff to do first."

"You want me to come with?"

It wasn't an unusual request, but it threw me. I was heading across the hall to find out what was supposed to be happening today and I didn't think having Clancy along was such a good idea.

"Why?"

Clancy shrugged. "I've got a few hours spare before I go to Jo's parents tonight for dinner, I was hoping you'd want company."

"I'm good."

"You sure?"

"Yep."

"Aren't you forgetting something?" Clancy asked suddenly as I reached for the door.

"Don't think so."

"Your camera?"

"I'm not taking it today."

He gasped. "Who are you and what have you done with the real Nova?"

"Funny." I rolled my eyes, then immediately wished I hadn't as I felt the rise of nausea.

"The only time you don't take your camera is when Kate has set…oh my goodness, you've got a date." His grin was huge.

"No, I don –."

"You do. Who is he? Please tell me for your sake that he's cute. Did Kate set you up again?"

"No, Kate did not set me up and I don't have a date."

"Uh huh. Where are you heading?"

"None of your business."

Grinning he started singing. "Nova's got a date, Nova's got a date."

"What are you? In primary school?" I muttered as I opened the door.

"Wait up. I'm coming with you."

"Like hell you are."

"Tell me where you're going."

"I'm going across the hall. Can you leave me alone now?"

"Kate'll have your hide if you're seeing Zeph."

"I've got eyes in my head, I can't help seeing him."

My comment made me aware again that my eyes didn't work as they should anymore. Kate had told Clancy about the apparent drugging and he'd been concerned, but not nearly as suffocating as Kate.

Thankfully, he didn't comment on my faux pas as he just about skipped to the door.

"It's the brother, isn't it? Please tell me it's the brother."

"Go away, Clancy."

"I'm standing at the door of my own unit, Nova." He grinned.

"Get back inside."

He leaned against the door jamb so I had no hope of closing the door. "It's a free country."

"You're embarrassing me."

"Why?" He winked. "You've got some fun stuff planned."

"Look…just…whatever."

Crossing the hallway, I knocked on the door. Zeph opened it and I glanced at the floor as he waved to Clancy.

"He's hoping I've got a date with Benaiah." I muttered under my breath.

Zeph grinned. "Hey Benny…" He called over his shoulder as he let me in. "Nova's here."

"Thanks a lot," I muttered sarcastically as I closed the door behind me.

Benaiah for his part, glanced up from his many computer monitors with a confused look. I came to a standstill as I saw that the room had three other people visiting. They were all Nephilim. Ransom, I knew. There was also a guy who was slender and slight, with pure white hair, which made him look pixie-esque. Hazy orange images formed above his head, quickly seeping from one image to the next. The other guy was of average size with a tubby tummy, receding blond hair and silver cogs etched into his skin.

Zeph gestured behind him as he sat next to the blond cog man. "Clancy was watching."

"So?" Benaiah shrugged.

"It's a great cover, man, besides it's about time you had a girlfriend."

I'm not sure who was more shocked at Zeph's blasé comment, but Benaiah won hands down in the embarrassment department. I could see the blush which stained his cheeks as he ducked his head.

I gave a small wave at the other guys who were still looking at me. "Hi."

"Nova, this is Tiberius…" Zeph pointed at the pixie followed by the cog man. "…and this is Magee."

Magee cleared his throat. "Can I see your eyes?"

"Magee, she's only just come through the door. Give her a moment would you?" Tiberius admonished in a very British accent.

"Sorry, it's simply that I've never seen pitch eyes on an adult before."

"Is it that weird?" I asked.

"No, no, not weird." Magee assured. "Simply…unusual."

"Weird." I clarified. "It's too bright in here to show you."

I caught the glance between them but Zeph explained before I could. "Photophobia."

"Is that because of the pitch?" Magee asked.

Zeph answered as he stood. "Not sure. Benny couldn't heal it, so perhaps."

"How many times do I have to tell you not to call me that?"

"Mom does."

"You're not Mom." Benaiah glared.

"And I'm glad for that." Zeph turned off the overhead lights.

Obviously, he had decided for me that I would parade my eyes like some sort of circus freak show. With a sigh, I slid my sunnies from my face and blinked a few times to adjust to the light. It was only the glow from the computer screens and the open doors to the other rooms but it was enough to need a second. Even Ransom crowded around me as four of the five Nephilim wanted a look. Only Benaiah stayed seated. I think Zeph was in his element acting like he was showing off his new toy. After a few minutes I'd had enough and replaced the sunnies without saying a word. Leaving them to discuss my eyes like a scientific marvel, I left the huddle and took the seat beside Benaiah. He gave me a quick smile then inclined his head toward them.

"They can be a bit much sometimes, but they mean well." He said quietly.

"I'm sure." I agreed as I glanced at the computer screens.

Even with the sunnies they were bright. One had a map of the city, one had drawings like blueprints and one had scrolling text.

"Are you some sort of hacker or something?"

"Or something." He nodded. "When you're on your own a lot, you pick up a few things."

I glanced at the guys as a chilling thought came to me. "You do realise the proof room is going to be dark, don't you?"

"And?"

"I'm not going to be able to wear my sunnies without raising questions. The minute Edward sees my eyes, the brown stuff is going to hit the oscillating rotator isn't it?"

Benaiah glanced at me for a second then raised his voice. "Guys, Nova has a good point."

Still talking amongst themselves, they didn't respond. Tucking his bottom lip a little into his mouth, Benaiah let out a piercing whistle. It was even enough to make me jump. He gave me a nod.

"How is Edward going to react when he sees my eyes? I can't wear my sunnies in the proof room."

From the sudden stillness it was obvious they hadn't thought about that. Finally, Zeph turned to Tiberius. "Your department, I think."

"I quite like a challenge. Would you remove your sunglasses again?"

I shifted the chair around until I was facing away from the screens and waited until Tiberius came around the table before doing so. There wasn't much room and I needed to scoot further to allow the English man some space. I ended up resting slightly against Benaiah's jean-clad leg. I thought he would stand and leave but he didn't move away.

"Do you mind if I touch you?" Tiberius asked.

"I guess not."

"Always prudent to ask, you know. Touching can lead to trouble. Let's see now." He gave a quick sigh and a grin. "This really is amazing."

"Yeah, I'm catching onto that. So what do you do?"

"I'm an illusionist." His fingers lightly held my face and he closed his eyes for a moment. His touch grew cool against my skin as the image above his head shifted into eyes. "I can work with this. What colour eyes would you like?"

"They're normally brown."

"Which shade?"

I shrugged. "Light brown."

"Like a good cognac." Benaiah said in a low voice.

Tiberius was in my line of vision but I glanced over without moving my head. Benaiah shifted and suddenly seemed to find something on his desk very interesting.

"If you would look at me please."

The English accented Apath interrupted my focus and I brought my gaze back to him. There was something so utterly endearing about Benaiah's shy smiles and the fact that he blushed.

"There we are. Nothing to it. But I think…" Tiberius slid my sunnies back on my face and paused a moment with his fingers lightly touching the sides. "There now. Nothing unusual to be seen is there? Go and have a look at yourself." Tiberius told me as he stood and moved away.

I went to the bathroom and used the mirror. I couldn't see anything different. I moved the sunnies out of the way and saw that nothing had changed. My eyes were still black.

"What am I supposed to be seeing?" I called out as I pushed the glasses back into place.

"Exactly." Tiberius showed up at the door. "You can still feel them."

"Feel what?"

"The sunglasses. Don't worry about misplacing them. This is the fun bit." Gesturing me out of the room Tiberius waited until I was closer then slid the glasses off. "Now you see them…" He slid them back on. "Now you don't."

Suddenly it clicked. Tiberius had apparently worked his Nephilim illusions to hide the sunnies and return my eyes to brown…except I couldn't see the illusion.

"Thank you."

"You are very welcome."

I went back to my seat as Tiberius returned to where Magee was explaining some sort of electronic device.

"Benaiah, what do you see?" I asked quietly.

"Sorry?"

"I feel like the kid in the crowd with the Emperor's New Clothes. I can't see the wonder." I moved the sunnies out of the way and squinted in his direction. "And they're still black."

"Of course. You can see through the illusion…and I wouldn't recommend doing that with those shades."

"What?"

He tapped the top of his head. "You've got this funky hair bump."

I quickly brought the glasses back down. "So what do you see?"

"You. Light brown eyes and I can't see the shades."

"Does the illusion work for everyone? I mean is that what everyone will see?"

"You're the only person I know who can see through abilities."

"Yes, well…I am exceptional."

"That you are."

Somehow, I don't think he meant to say that out loud.

"Benny." Zeph interrupted. "You're up."

Benaiah cleared his throat and moved his hands to the keyboard. "There's been no increase in activity around Nova's studio as far as I can see.

"It's not really my studio. I just hire it occasionally."

"Yeah, we know." Zeph said offhandedly.

"The only people who have been there is Tracy Godwin who owns the studio, Deborah Miles who came in to have photos taken. She wasn't left alone for more than a few minutes but she didn't do any apparent snooping. The same for Rachel Markus who wasn't left alone at all, and then there was the Shane family. Wendy, Brent, and daughter Gail. I couldn't see any obvious snooping either." Benaiah shrugged.

"What about on the outside?" Ransom's low voice rumbled.

"If there was a Nephilim within a ten block radius of the studio, they didn't flag. I don't think there's been any movement. These guys are being more careful than what we've come to expect from them…or they're not preparing for anything at all."

I frowned at Benaiah's report. This all sounded very movie-esque. "How do you know all that?"

Magee scratched his head. "We…may have gone in yesterday and set some things up."

"You what? What sort of things."

"Surveillance, cameras…you know, the usual."

I stared at all of them, one at a time. "You're serious?"

"I did say you wouldn't be alone with him." Zeph shrugged.

I took in a steadying breath. "Okay, suddenly I find myself in an episode of the Avengers."

"Sweet." Magee laughed. "Does that mean I'm Iron Man?"

Zeph threw a scrunched paper ball at him. "If you were green you'd be the Incredible Bulk."

"Wow. Did you think that up by yourself or did someone write it for you?" Magee shot back.

"Witty. If you had more than half a brain cell, you'd be dangerous."

"Gentlemen…" Tiberius cut in. "We do have a lady present. Have a little decorum."

"I've got decorum." Magee quipped. "What do you think I wash my hair in?"

I snorted at that, but I don't think anyone else got the joke.

"Perhaps the masses require feeding before they revolt." Ransom suggested.

"Too late for that. They're already revolting," I told him.

Suddenly a paper ball hit my chest. Picking it up, I threw it back at Zeph. He rippled and it sailed right though him.

"That's cheating.

He rippled a second time. "It's using my talents."

"I'm surrounded by children." Benaiah muttered as he shook his head.

His wry comment didn't stop him from retaliating when Zeph threw another ball of paper.

Chapter Ten

"Hi, Nova."

"Hey, Tracy. How's it going?"

"Busy. Three sittings today, can you believe it? Our advertising blitz must be working."

"Must be."

I hoped like heck I was acting normally. It was one thing to know that no one else would be able to see Zeph, it was another thing entirely to believe it when I saw him walking at my side.

"Is it free?" I pointed towards the proofing room.

"All yours, mate."

"Thanks. And sorry about the short notice."

"No sweat."

Opening the door, I let Zeph in first then went to the console to load the photos.

He shimmered. "You weren't kidding about it being a dark room."

I flicked the switch for the down lights and saw his shadow. Quickly I shut the door. "What are you doing?"

"I can't talk when I'm invisible and Edward will hear the Apath and know something's up. So why is it so dark in here?"

"It helps to see the images when they're projected."

"Like a movie theatre."

"Something like that." I navigated the program and soon the pictures were displayed on the wall. "Describe Edward to me."

"Why?"

"Because all I can see is a guy with blond hair and silver quills."

"Ugh." Zeph pulled a face. "Blond hair, kind of spiky…ironically. Light eyes, blue maybe, Caucasian, fairly average looking, I suppose."

I waited but he appeared finished. "That's a lot of help."

"What do you want from me? I'm a guy. I don't usually run around classifying other guys in descriptive terms."

A buzz sounded at the console. I hit the intercom and Tracy's voice came over the speaker. "A Mr Edward Huber to see you."

I glanced at my watch. "At least he's punctual. Showtime."

"Nova?"

"Yeah?"

"Relax. He's just any other client for photos."

Benaiah had already told me the same thing as we left the unit but it didn't help. My heart pounded as I opened the door and headed for the foyer. I wiped my sweaty palms on my jeans, took a breath and plastered on a smile.

"Edward. Hi." I tried to imagine, or even remember, average looking Caucasian male.

"Hello."

He reached a hand toward me and I indicated the way instead. "Follow me. This shouldn't take long."

"Nice." Edward said as he entered the room. "Quite a set up."

I shrugged and quickly glanced at Zeph. He was wearing a set of glasses that I knew had a camera attached. "We make do. Now the photos will show up on the wall over there. Take your time and we can move through them as often as you like. Would you like to sit or stand?"

"Standing's fine."

"Great."

From behind the console, I controlled the slide show. It only took about a minute to show all five and by that time Zeph had circled him twice.

"Were there any more than this?"

"None that were any good. I scrapped the rest."

"I can't really decide. You take good photos."

"Thanks. Would you like me to go through them again?"

"No. I'll take numbers one and three if that's okay?"

"No problem. I can have them ready next week. Do you want them posted?"

"I'll collect them if that's alright by you."

"I'll give you a call when they are ready."

It was over. I could barely sleep last night for worrying and it was over in less than ten minutes.

"Actually, there was something else before I go."

My heart hit overdrive and I hoped I sounded casual. "Sure?"

Edward smiled and slid his fingers into the front pockets of his trousers. "Would you like to go out for a coffee sometime…or ice cream?"

I made a strangled sound in shock and I couldn't think. "What?"

Zeph made an immediate move to the communication thingy in his ear then frantically shook his head.

Edward flexed his knees and shrugged. "I was hoping we could get together sometime. It wouldn't have to be a date or anything. You could ask your friend, Kate, along."

"Um…I'll have to see what my boyfriend thinks of that."

"You have a boyfriend? Of course you do…" He laughed. "…someone as pretty as you would have a boyfriend. Look, please don't think…anyway, it was nice meeting you again and I'll wait for the call about the photos."

I looked down at the console and busied myself with removing the card from the drive as I saw his hand come up for a handshake again. Calming a little, I gave him another smile as he continued to stand there.

"I'll just…show you out."

I flicked off the lights and hurried to the door, leaving it open so Zeph could follow. Not that he needed it, I suppose. He could have walked through it.

"Nova, about before, please don't think…I'm sorry if I caused you…well, you can't fault me for taste right?"

Zeph mimed vomiting, which made me laugh. "No. It's fine. Thanks for coming in."

Edward offered his hand again but this time I didn't have an excuse.

"I won't bite." He laughed.

"The last time we did this you got me with static electricity."

"If you remember, that was the time before."

"Fine." Hesitantly, I held out my hand. His hand touched mine and I yanked it back fast as pain hit my palm. "Ow, you got me again."

Edward did a completely believable job of acting incredulous while I almost had a heart attack as Benaiah appeared out of the shadows. When Edward didn't react to him I realised that Benaiah was somehow invisible. Possibly with Tiberius' help.

I cupped my hands together so it didn't look strange when Benaiah held it.

"I don't believe it. Twice. That never happens. It goes to show that there are sparks between us."

I shook my head as I saw the rainbow aura sink into my hand. "I'm not shaking hands a fourth time, just remember that. You can keep your sparks to yourself."

Edward laughed. "I'll talk to you later about the photos, Nova. Take care now."

I waited until the front door closed behind him. "It felt like the shunt thing Ransom has."

"Sorry?"

Glancing behind me, I saw Tracy come out from the office. "Nothing, just talking to myself."

"He was cute."

"Ugh…" I groaned. "…you can have him."

"Bit full of himself?"

"And then some."

"Looked like he might be. That was quick." She thumbed towards the proofing room.

"I think the whole exercise was to ask me on a date."

"Oh, things looking up, hey?"

I snorted. "If he comes sniffing around again, tell him I have a boyfriend."

"I'd love to. How 'bout you help the story and actually get yourself one?"

"You and Kate. You're both the same."

"I want you to be happy, hon."

Benaiah released me and I dropped my hand and the banter. "Gotta run."

"Of course you do. No charge for today. I don't charge in five minute blocks."

"You're a sweetheart. See you."

Out on the street I pulled out my phone so I didn't look daft talking to myself.

"Well?"

Benaiah shook his head. "Nothing. He definitely pierced your skin but I couldn't detect anything else."

"What? Benaiah, what are you doing here?"

I quickly glanced around the street when I heard Zeph's voice. It was a little disconcerting not knowing if I was supposed to be able to see him, but since he once again had a shadow, I just hoped no one else had seen him appear from mid-air.

"I was worried Edward would pull a stunt like this. Obviously I was right."

"Where the hell are you?" Zeph demanded.

"Now you know what it feels like."

"Guys, we've got other things to worry about at the moment." I glanced at Benaiah. "How can you tell he didn't add extra genes?"

"Extra would still be foreign to your body that soon after injection."

"Maybe he didn't add, maybe he took. Like I said, it felt like the shunt thing of Ransom's."

Zeph tilted his head for a moment and I could tell he was listening. "Ransom says it's possible. If he took a sample of your blood, Benny wouldn't sense that."

I saw Benaiah's brief glare but he didn't comment about his brother's use of the pet name as Zeph's expression changed to shock. "Ransom told me that if he did take blood, Edward's going to know you're a Nephilim by the time you phone him about the photos."

"Doesn't something like that take weeks?"

"Only if you work for the government. And remember, Lauder is a genealogical scientist…or whatever it's called. He'll have the facilities Edward needs."

"Oh hell."

Benaiah placed a hand on my back as I swayed. "We'll work it out. Don't worry."

"I'll work on the photos tonight, it won't take long. I forgot to ask what size he wanted them in but five-by-eights should be fine. I'll call him tomorrow, tell him it didn't take as long as I thought. He can't have blood results that fast right?"

Zeph gave a sharp nod. "You work on the photos and we'll keep an eye on where he's heading."

"Did everything work out with tracking him?"

"Like clockwork. Magee's got him on screen now. Even if that's supposed to be Benaiah's job. Tiberius, what were you thinking giving him cover like that?"

I couldn't hear the response but it didn't make Zeph look any happier.

"It's not up to you to put him in danger."

"No…" Benaiah muttered. "…that's your job."

"Okay." I put my phone away. "I'll let you two fight it out. I'm heading home to work on some photos."

Chapter Eleven

Groaning, I snaked a hand out to smite my alarm. It wasn't working. It was only as I peered out from under my pillow that I registered the sound was coming from my phone. Fumbling with the covers, I brought the handset under the pillow with me.

"Hello?"

"Nova, it's Tracy. Just wanted to tell you Edward Huber picked up the photos this morning."

"Um….okay." I breathed. "Thanks."

"You okay?"

"I was asleep."

"Late night?"

"Possibly. What time is it?"

"A touch after eleven."

"In the morning?" I heard her laugher. It was too cheerful for the way I was feeling. "Love you too, Trace." I grumbled into the mattress.

"You artist types are all the same you know."

I groaned and hung up the phone. Normally, Tracy was right. My routine was to go to sleep to the sun and wake up at the crack of noon. The last few days though I was so tired, my body ached and I was always cold. I told Kate and Clancy I had the flu. I think they believed me.

As for Edward, I was glad it was now over. He had no reason to contact me further. I'd had the photos done and dusted and down to Tracy's studio the day after his last visit. My friendly neighbourhood Nephilim had warned me from meeting him a third time and I whole heartedly agreed. No more quill pricks for me thank you very much. Now, two weeks later he finally picked up the photos.

Closing my eyes in an effort to go back to sleep, I jerked up in bed as I remembered today's date. Dizzy, I dropped back onto the pillow. I hated being sick but that wasn't going to stop me from what I needed to do today. Normally I could be ready to go anywhere in twenty minutes. Forty-five minutes later I was shivering, sweating and struggling to put on my shoes.

If it wasn't Aiden's birthday, I think I would have stayed cocooned in bed. I'd made a promise to think of him on his birthday. Traditionally, I would go to the cemetery and talk to him but since the church was closer I decided to go there instead. It still took nearly an hour to get to the church and I was exhausted by the time I arrived. Thankful for the pew, I sank down onto the hard, wooden bench. It was a struggle to breathe and my throat burned with every breath. Despite the flu shot I'd had earlier in the year, maybe I really was coming down with the virus.

After a few moments I went over to where they had their candles. Selecting one, I lit it from another candle and set it into the large bronze bowl of sand.

"Happy Birthday, Aiden." I whispered. "What a year it's been. You wouldn't believe me if you tried. Actually, most of it you would, it's only the past few weeks that have been doozies. Miss you heaps." Tears filled my eyes as I repeated one of the last things he'd said to me. "At least I know you'll be there with the welcome mat when I finally get to heaven."

Wiping my cheeks, I sat back on the pew and glanced for a Bible. There weren't any. Since the church was directly opposite one of the largest train stations in the city I wasn't too surprised. Pulling out my phone I tapped the Bible app and scrolled to Jeremiah and Aiden's favourite verse. I could have quoted by memory but there was something comforting in seeing the words.

"For I know the plans I have for you, declares the Lord, plans for good and not to harm you, to give you a future and a hope."

Despite celebrating six birthdays without him, in my memory Aiden would always remain nineteen. I'd always thought it ironic that the boy who'd had no future here on earth had hung onto the verse about having a future…and a hope. Knowing him, he would have got it.

By the time I boarded the tram and gratefully accepted the seat offered by a kind gentleman, I was shaking, aching all over and could hear a wheeze in my laboured breathing. The sooner I could get to bed the happier I would be.

I didn't make it.

Squeezing my eyes shut, I pressed my hand to my mouth to quell the rise of nausea. I was feeling hot then cold and I was starting to sweat. Groaning, I pressed a shaky hand to the console to code me into my building. I couldn't get my hand to function properly and my arm felt so heavy and tired. Stumbling inside, I collapsed on the bench which lined the wall under the mailboxes. I wasn't sure how this Apath thing worked but right now I was willing to give anything a go which didn't require movement.

"Benaiah. Help."

I felt the thought push its way through the chilled honey-like barrier. Holding myself still, I waited a moment, trying not to throw up.

"Nova, what's wrong? Where are you?"

The moment of relief was overshadowed by the agonising pain in my head and neck as I heard his voice. Breathing out hard, I had to wait for a while. The pain didn't ease.

"Sick...foyer."

Gripping the edge of the bench, I felt so dizzy I nearly passed out. In fact, I would have welcomed it. My limbs flared with heat and I went completely numb. Losing my balance I felt myself slide from the chair. I think I hit my head on the something. Flashes of light scrambled across my vision but everything else was black. I couldn't feel anything but pain. A huge weight pressed against my chest and iron bands squeezed my body. I couldn't breathe. For the first time in a long time there was complete darkness. It was almost a relief to surrender to it.

Slowly, a warm rainbow filled my head and I was floating. The rainbow swirled gently around me until I felt more like myself. The numbness was replaced by tingles and gradually I could feel again. Feeling as though I was surfacing from under water, I took a great gasping breath as I opened my eyes. Benaiah's aura was running through my skin as though he was using a strong wind to guide it. Both his hands held mine.

"There you are." He smiled softly. "I thought I'd lost you for a minute."

"I…"

"Shhh, give me a little longer, just to be sure."

I wasn't about to argue. Closing my eyes again, I let the warmth from his aura soothe me. After a few moments I became aware that his knees were on either side of my thighs and he was straddling me. There was plenty of space between us and he sat closer to my knees than anywhere, but it was still disconcerting. Particularly when I realised my hands were resting on his thighs.

"Okay." He whispered. "I think we're past the worst of it now, but there is still a ways to go. Do you feel okay now?"

"Uh huh." I gave an affirmative sound, not sure I could trust my voice at that precise moment.

"Do you think you'll be able to move?"

"Uh huh."

Keeping one hand captured, he lifted himself away from me then helped me into a sitting position.

"I feel so weak." I admitted with a groan as I tried to move.

"That'll happen when you stop breathing. Hold on."

Benaiah manoeuvred into a position which allowed him to pick me up. He really was as strong as he looked. Carrying me didn't affect a groan, grunt or laboured breathing and I'm not the most petite thing

around. I laid my head against his chest and wrapped
an arm around his neck to make it easier for him. It
still boggled my mind that he could heal. I felt like a
dishcloth, weak and limp but all the other pains,
aches, fever and nausea had disappeared.

Benaiah carried me into their unit.

"You leave your door open?" I asked as he
shouldered it further then kicked it shut behind him.

"I was in a hurry."

"Sorry."

"Don't be. It's okay."

Without letting me go, he fell back onto the sofa. I
didn't even know they had a sofa. I let out a small
squeak of surprise which ended when we landed
safely. He kept one hand at my back and removed the
one from under my legs to take hold of mine at his
chest. Sprawled across his lap and cradled in his
arms…this felt a lot more intimate than before, but I
wasn't about to complain.

I ordered my brain into gear. "Did Edward inject
something after all?"

I felt Benaiah shake his head behind me. "My best
guess is that your body is still fighting the gene."

"Best guess?"

"It's complicated."

"I'm not going anywhere."

He shifted a little and gently placed me closer to
the arm of the chair. I think he needed circulation
back in his arm.

"Zeph doesn't know this, but I have come across
humans who have been injected with our genes
before. The first reaction the human body has is to
treat it like a virus and attack it. Only because of what

it is, the Nephilim gene fights back and it creates
Nephilim cells in the body. These cells crowd out the
human cells and because there is now a lack of space
inside, the human cells can't reproduce."

His description made a sinking connection. "Like
leukaemia."

"I don't know. I've never healed someone with
leukaemia. I don't know what it feels like. I've tried
healing this in the other people, but once the
Nephilim cells start they are always there. I can only
remove so much. Because their body keeps producing
human cells there is always a war going on inside. I
could only give momentary relief. In your case, it's
different."

"Different how?"

"Your body started to attack the gene but when I
healed you that first time it stopped the attack,
allowing the Nephilim gene to be absorbed by your
body and attach itself to your DNA. The new cells in
your body are like those of us who are born Nephilim
but your remaining human cells are still treating those
new cells as the enemy."

"So when the last of my human cells die?"

"Then I think that would mean you stop getting
sick. At least like this."

My human side was going to die. It was a good
thing I'd accepted the whole Nephilim idea because
while this was freaking me out a little, I wasn't going
into total shock over it.

"So, because you healed me that first night,
Edward and his bunch have actually succeeded in
creating their first Nephilim?"

"Yeah." Benaiah sighed. "And that's why I haven't told Zeph, because if my theory is right…it's my fault."

I looked up at him. "Don't blame yourself, Benaiah. You didn't know this was going to happen."

"No, but I should have realised what the foreign body in your system was. I've felt the Nephilim gene often enough."

"Really? From what you said, you've only felt the gene after it's exploded into cells."

"I…" With a frown he stopped talking, his eyes moving as he thought. "I suppose you're right."

A comfortable silence fell between us as one of his hands lightly caressed my back through my clothes and the other gently held my hand.

Suddenly, what he'd said earlier clicked. "You said I wasn't breathing? Did you bring me back from the dead?"

He rocked his head. "Even I can't do that."

"This is draining you, isn't it? Maybe you should stop now."

"Shh. I'm fine."

"Benaiah—"

"I said I was fine. Now can we sit here for a little while and pretend to be normal?"

"Sure." I quipped. "We'll be normal while you sit here and heal me."

"Shush."

With a sigh, I closed my eyes and relaxed against him. His arm came around my shoulders and he simply held me. Slowly, realisation dawned and I understood what he'd meant by normal. Benaiah couldn't touch someone without healing them. It was more than likely he'd never held a girl in his arms, but that was something normal guys did. I liked that it was me he was holding. Gently, I threaded my fingers though his. He moved his hand to accommodate me but didn't say a word. Encouraged, I closed my eyes, removed my sunnies and dropped my head to his shoulder as I wrapped my free arm around his back.

"Comfy?" He asked.

"Yeah. You?"

"Absolutely."

"Benaiah. What's going on? Do you need back up?"

I nearly jumped a mile when I heard Zeph's voice in my head.

"Take it easy, Zeph. She's okay. Not quite out of the woods yet, but getting there."

"What's going on?"

Benaiah gave an edited version of the 'body fighting the gene' theory that he'd given me. I kept quiet as I listened to his heartbeat near my ear. My body was killing itself. Mad scientists had turned me into a lab rat. I had wicked night vision but couldn't take photos. My world was on its head and I found comfort and peace in the arms of a man who couldn't touch people. That sounded just about right.

Chapter Twelve

"Isn't it private? I mean it's mind-speak right?"

Benaiah sat on my office chair with his hands clasped loosely between his knees, while I sat hugging a cushion in my La-Z-Boy across the room. We were supposed to be looking at photos of Nephilim, with me explaining what I could see and Benaiah telling me what their actual abilities were. The whole idea was to help me identify abilities from what I saw. According to Zeph, the Spiderman philosophy applied to being a Nephilim. With great power comes great responsibility and apparently one of those responsibilities was to learn to use your power. Even if it was classified as a 'passive' one, like mine. I also think Zeph pushed us to have these pow-wows at my place because he was having a lot of fun with the idea that his brother was spending time—alone—in the company of a girl. It didn't mean that Benaiah suddenly became 'touchy-feely' with me. Quite the opposite. His moment of 'normality' the other night seemed to be the limit between us. Whenever we met, he would briefly take my hand to judge the balance of cells…and that was it. I wasn't surprised even if it was slightly disappointing.

At the moment though, I wanted to know about Apath.

"It's basically speaking normally but in a way humans can't pick up." Benaiah answered without looking up from his hands. "There are two sorts of Apath. Indirect and direct."

"Okay?" I urged when he fell silent.

"I may need help to explain this…*Zeph, are you free? I want to show Nova the difference in Apath.*"

"*Shoot.*"

He glanced at me. "So you heard that right?"

"Yes."

"That was indirect. Normal conversation. Anyone within a certain radius can hear us. Now I'm going to concentrate on Zeph specifically."

I waited. I felt a slight pushing on the chilled-honey barrier I'd come to associate with Apath, but it was like hearing someone speaking quietly on the other side of a door.

"So what did you hear then?" I told him and he nodded. "Zeph could hear me clearly, while you heard a mumbled whisper. If you listen closely when that happens you can make out some of what is being said but there's a sort of unwritten etiquette that says doing so is rude. You're supposed to let those slide by without attempting to eavesdrop. Some people are really rude though."

I gave a chuckle, but it made sense. "That's why Zeph didn't want to Apath when Edward was near. He would have dropped eaves."

Benaiah let out a soft laugh. "Exactly. If you notice, our group doesn't usually Apath."

"I've heard you doing it, though."

Benaiah nodded. "Normally you get a group of Nephilim together and no one speaks…" He moved his hand to indicate actual vocal speaking. "…Apath is our thing, I suppose. We're brought up doing it so sometimes we slip up, or we do it deliberately when we need to say something we don't want humans to hear. But since we want to keep low key, we talk most of the time."

"And you want to keep low key because of Edward and his cronies?"

That made him quirk that sexy half-smile of his. "Yes."

"So how do I concentrate on a particular person?"

"When you think of someone, you don't always see them in your mind like you see them in person, do you? Normally it's a flash or a memory, right?"

"I guess so." I shrugged.

"It's kind of like that word association game. If I gave you a name what's the first thing that comes into your head? Kate."

"Teasing wink."

"Zeph."

"Wings."

"Benaiah."

"Shy smile, warm rainbow."

There was an instant silence between us as he ducked his head with a breath of laughter.

"Brat," I told him as I threw the cushion. He easily caught it. I shifted in the chair. "So what do you see when you think of me?"

He blushed and I was intrigued. "Smiling eyes that can see into my soul."

That took my breath away. "Black?"

"Light brown."

"Like cognac." I smiled.

I didn't think it was possible for him to blush any redder but he did. Clearing his throat, he looked down at the cushion then passed it back without looking at me.

"Anyway, you bring that to mind as you Apath…and it…um…sends it to that person."

"So you have to know the person first?"

Benaiah nodded.

"That makes sense."

I watched him for a moment as he continued to stare at his hands. He was the sweetest, shyest man I'd ever met. I suppose the dates Kate had pushed me on didn't work because the guys were all macho-alpha males who damn well knew it. There was something about Benaiah that drew me to him. Like a moth to the flame. I could tell, that if anything were to happen between us…it would be up to me. Taking that step wasn't easy and my stomach clenched at the thought of it. Since Aiden's death I hadn't really let myself get that close to people. It hurt too much. But with Benaiah, I found myself wanting to try.

Hesitantly, I slid from the chair to the floor and knelt at his feet so I could get him to look at me. His beautiful green eyes flicked my way and returned to his hands. Almost as if he couldn't help himself, Benaiah glanced at me again. This time he didn't look away.

I placed my hand on his jean-clad calf. "I like you, too."

His lips parted as he breathed out hard. He licked his lips then swallowed. After a moment, he lifted his hand, moving it to my face but hovered just beyond touch. His eyes closed on a sigh as his hand dropped to my shoulder.

"I have to fight it, Nova. I can't…I'll never have a…a real…I'm classified as an Active-Untouchable for a reason." His eyes opened and I could see the struggle he was having with himself. "Untouchables can't have normal lives. Our abilities will destroy us…or the other person. It's easier for me not to get involved with anyone. I'll never hurt you but—"

"But touching me can hurt you," I finished for him.

"I'm sorry." He whispered.

There was pain in his eyes. I couldn't help myself. Rising to my knees, I moved around until I could wrap my arms around his waist. I rested my head on his side. His hand snaked around my shoulder and he held me closer to him. Abruptly, he moved. The chair wheeled backwards into the desk while he was suddenly on the floor with me, crushing me to his chest with a groan. Both of us were fully clothed and I could feel his hands on my back.

"This is suicide. Absolute suicide." He muttered. "You don't make things any easier."

"Sorry." I whispered. Perhaps I should have moved away but I didn't want to.

"You smell good." His voice was low and it made me laugh a little. "And you feel great."

From behind us came the sound of a throat clearing. We pulled apart and I saw Kate at the door. The door, which until then had been shut.

"Ever heard of knocking?" I glared.

"Yep, heard of it, but it's overrated when I get to see the most interesting of things. If you two lovebirds can bear to be separated, grub's up."

She left the door open as she vacated the doorway. I glanced at Benaiah and saw the blush. "Subtlety is not her strong suit."

"It's for the best."He told me as he stood. "It's a path we shouldn't be taking. I should be going, anyway." With a half-smile he looked down at me. "I want to help you up."

"Do you trust me?"

"I suppose."

"Well, hold out your hand."

We both had long sleeves on, so when he held out his hand I grabbed his wrist. He grabbed mine too and pulled me to my feet.

I smiled at him. "See, it's not all bad."

"Giving in to temptation is always a bad thing."

Dropping my wrist, he looked at me for a moment then turned and walked out of the room. By the time I followed, the front door was closing behind him.

"Was it something I said?" Kate asked as I walked over to the counter.

"It's your knack for creating embarrassing moments." Clancy came to my rescue. "I told you, you should knock first."

"So…you and Ben, hey?" Kate gave a knowing look. "I knew there had to be something. You never invite anyone into your office to work on photos."

"He has a good eye."

"Good eye, good bod, good muscles, great butt." She winked at me with a grin. "So spill the goss. Is he as good a kisser as I imagine him to be?"

That made me look at her. "You imagine kissing Benaiah?"

She shrugged. "He's cute."

"You keep your thoughts to yourself." I told her.

Kate gave a squeal. "This is so exciting. You've got a boyfriend."

"I don't…" I stopped talking when I saw her face. I'd fallen for it hook, line and sinker. I changed tack to cover. "…kiss and tell."

"Let her be, Kate. New love is a tender thing."

I snorted. "It's not…"

"There doesn't have to be an official announcement for love to blossom. From what I saw, give it a few days and you'll update your status all on your lonesome." Kate patted my hand.

"She's not lonesome, Kate, she's got Benaiah now. Remember?"

"Just pass the food," I scowled.

Clancy handed me a plate of chicken salad as I picked up the fork from the bench.

"So are you going to walk me to work today?" Kate asked, thankfully changing the subject.

"I'm out." Clancy told her. "Jo's coming around."

"Nova?"

"Why would I do that?"

"So we can talk, make fun of strangers, have a few laughs."

"So you can keep having digs at me about Benaiah. No, thank you."

She held up her hand. "I won't. I promise. Besides it's been forever since you got out of the house. The roof doesn't count."

Cocking my head, I thought about it. "It's only been ten days."

"Oh, yeah? Not including the one trip to the optometrist to get your new sunnies, how long has it been?"

"Four weeks." I muttered, shoving chicken salad into my mouth.

"Only four weeks? What was I thinking? That's no time at all. Seriously, Nova, you're a hermit."

"And you're pushy."

"So what else is new? And you're not bringing your camera."

"You're bossy, too."

"I know…" She grabbed my arm and hugged it. "But aren't I delightful?"

Shaking my head at her antics, I let her bully me around. After lunch, I walked with her to the tram stop. She was right. It had been a while since I'd left the building. I didn't want to go too far with Edward around armed with the knowledge of my changing bloodline. Despite the gang of four Nephilim keeping tabs on the area, no one had seen him or his friends. A trip to the Labyrinth should be fine. All the same, I concentrated on Benaiah and Apathed where I was going. Better safe than sorry. I chose to Apath him directly because I wanted to add an addendum to the information.

"Are we okay? Still friends?"

"Heck, yes."

"What are you laughing at?" Kate demanded.

"I wasn't laughing."

"Well, you snorted in humour then."

"If you could only read my mind." I waggled my eyebrows at her.

"Hell, no, there would be a ghost in a wishing well or whatever the heck it is."

We both laughed causing a few people to both smile and scowl at us. I didn't care.

I travelled the rest of the way with Kate and saw her off at the Labyrinth, declining a coffee. Shoving my hands into the back pockets of my jeans, despite my wallet, I started walking home. It would take longer but it was a beautiful day; a touch on the cool side but okay with my jacket once I started walking. With a smile, I headed down the street and angled my way to the park.

Chapter Thirteen

"Hi. Nova, isn't it?"

I glanced behind me at the sound of my name then stumbled as my heart went into overdrive. I gave a nod but kept walking.

Viola matched my step. "I thought so. Fancy meeting you here."

"I had a meeting." I finally managed. The others had warned me about giving any indication as to where I lived or any part of my routine. Glancing at her, I ran what I could see against what Benaiah and I had figured out. She had a red glow at her throat. It came out in puffs when she spoke, but not when she breathed.

A glow seemed to indicate an ability that wasn't physical. Warm colours…like red, was most likely an ability to control something. Location was throat. So what? Breath? No, too high. That would have been her lungs. Throat? Voice. Yes.

Oh crap. If I'd figured it out correctly, she could control people with her voice.

"You don't remember me do you?"

I gave a nod. "Sure. You're Edward's friend."

"Yes, I am." She smiled. "And you're going to come with me."

At the words 'come with me' the red glowing puff sped towards me like a hungry monster. It spread until it encased my torso from my shoulders to my knees.

"What the…?" This time my stumble had Nephilim help as my body suddenly came to a stop. With a smile, Viola turned and started walking the way we'd come. With jerky strides, my body involuntary followed. I felt like a zombie.

"What are you doing? Let me go."

"I'm not touching you." Viola pointed out, all wide-eyed and innocent. "But while we're on that subject, you can be quiet as well."

The red glow headed for my mouth.

"It'll be easier if you don't struggle. Trust me."

For a moment I could feel my panic nearly overwhelm me as the red glow came at me again before calmness settled and I figured I could trust her. I took a breath and walked a little faster to catch up. It was a nice day. Looking down at myself, I saw the red glow again. Most of my mind wanted to just follow meekly, stay quiet and trust her but the part of my mind that could understand what she was doing rebelled. I pulled my hand from my pocket and let it hang at my side. I could move it away from the glow. When I passed a pole, I gripped it and used it to plant my feet. I think I nearly broke my back as half of me continued walking while the other half of me refused to move. Gritting my teeth, I hung onto the pole for dear life as my feet tried to follow her. She hadn't stopped. She was calmly walking on as though I was following like a well-trained puppy. Moving backwards I planted my feet against the pole.

I glared down at the glow around me. I wanted to tell it to go away, to leave me alone, but I couldn't talk. Without thinking, I collected the image in my mind, not of Viola, but of the red glow and Apathed to it.

"I can see what you are and what you're doing. You have no power over me. Now let me go."

I staggered backwards as it obeyed me. For a split second I stood there, stunned, but when I heard Viola cry out, I spun and ran. A missile of some sort came from the left. I dropped to the ground as it sailed over the top of me. Scrambling to my feet, I started running again. I needed to get somewhere public.

"She's heading for the street. Cut her off now." Viola Apathed.

She wasn't alone. I swore as I tried to run faster. Weeks of inactivity was my weakness now. Another missile came at me and I jerked behind a tree, gasping for breath as the air burned next to my head when it went past. It felt cold, whatever it was.

"Tree."

"I've got her."

I recognised Edward from his Apath as I bolted from the tree, further into the park. I didn't get very far. A heavy body tackled me from behind and I crash landed, face first into a mouthful of dirt and leaves. I struggled like mad, opened my mouth and let out a scream. I felt a sharp sting in my back but I didn't stop struggling.

"Shut her up would you?"

"I'm trying."

I felt a second sting and kept struggling. My arms and legs began to feel weak but I wasn't giving up until I was down and out. A third sting came and suddenly the world spun and my body went limp. I couldn't move. I could still feel Edward on top of me.

"She's a fighter, I'll give her that." The Apath was almost admiring.

"How the hell did she resist my voice? That's what I want to know."

"I swear she dodged my ice-fire."

Ice. It made sense. The third guy from that night had frost-like skin.

Edward snorted. *"She tripped. Now pick her up will you?"*

"Seriously? Me?"

"I hope you're not defying orders, Julius."

"I thought you wanted her alive."

"I gave her three shots, but if she can get past Viola, she might get past that. Put her in hibernation would you?

The weight on my back disappeared and I felt hands turning me onto my back. I couldn't protect my eyes from the bright sunlight through the trees as I stared up at the shadowed figure.

"Poor pet." Julius whispered as he ran gloved fingers over my forehead before closing my eyes with his hand. "I bet you don't even know what's going on. Three shots of paralysis serum. He's mad."

I heard movement then felt his hand slide under my shirt to my chest. My heart rate didn't change but my panic levels hit the roof. I couldn't move to fight him off.

"How about I merely make you a touch cold? It'll be our little secret."

If I could have gasped I would have, as cold flared from his hand though my body.

"There now. That wasn't so bad was it?"

He removed his hand and pulled my shirt back down. Despite the freeze through my body I could still feel his cold touch as his fingers once again ran over my face.

"Such a pretty little thing. No wonder Edward broke the rules for you."

I felt cold on my lips and realised the damn prick had kissed me. Perhaps I should have stayed quiet but I wasn't going to let him get off that lightly.

"Go…to…hell." I breathed against his lips.

He took in a slow breath right next to my ear. "Oh, you beautiful thing. Keep fighting. Are these yours? Yes, that's right you were wearing shades."

Julius took a moment, from the sound of it, to replace his glove then lifted me into his arms.

"What took you so long?" Viola demanded as I heard a sliding sound. It sounded like a side door of a van.

"There's a fine line between hibernation and death, Sweetpea, should I have rushed it?"

"Get in the damn car."

Julius laid me on something then secured me with straps across my body. The car rocked as he got in and the door slid shut behind him. Obviously the paralysis serum only worked on the body and not the mind. I wasn't muddled or drowsy, I just couldn't move. I heard the drone of the engine as we headed out and I could hear traffic and noises of the city. It was impossible to tell which direction we were going. I was still capable of Apath but doing so would give me away immediately. It would be better to let them think I didn't know anything.

"It's Edward. We've got her. We're bringing her in."

There was no tug at the chilled-honey barrier in my mind. He'd obviously rung in somewhere…so either he'd broken the road rules and used a mobile phone while driving, or Viola was in the driver's seat. We drove for what felt like hours. The sounds of the city faded away as did any close traffic, and still we travelled. Finally, we stopped. My senses went on high alert as I tried to pinpoint something. Anything.

Petrol. I could smell petrol. The car rocked and a second later the sliding door opened.

"*Check on her.*" Edward's sudden Apath would have made me jump if I'd been capable of it.

"*Do you really think my abilities are that weak?*"

"*If she escapes, I'm holding you responsible.*"

"*So if she escapes after three shots of serum that's my fault?*"

The door slammed.

"*Somebody needs to take some chill pills.*"

"*Just do it, Julius.*" Viola sighed then added under her breath. "It's not worth the headache."

Another door opened and the car rocked again. If I was lying with my head away from the sliding door like it sounded, then Viola was definitely driving. I don't know why that mattered but it felt like I managed something meaningful by figuring that out.

The car rocked again and I heard Julius move closer.

"Alright, pet, let's take a look at you. You still with me?" He pressed his fingers to my face. "Hmm, a little warm. Don't want you to give me away, do we?"

Two of the three straps across my body clicked and I felt the tension release. His hand slid under my shirt and the freeze came again. When I could move again I was going to hit him with something. The harder and heavier, the better.

He snapped the straps back into place and caressed my face. "You really are pretty with a touch of colour in your cheeks but we can't have that, can we?"

Julius slid his hand to cup my jaw then lightly pressed his cold lips to mine again. I wondered…if I'd been a guy, would he be doing something else to cover his tracks.

"So, are you still with me?" He asked against my mouth.

I didn't respond this time. He brought his lips back to mine. It was a gentle kiss but the invasion of his tongue went too far. I growled at him. It wasn't much, more of husky rush of air but he pulled away and I could hear the smile in his voice.

"I knew you were there. Keep fighting, pet."

The sound of movement came again as did the rock of the car, followed shortly thereafter by the slide of the door.

"Well?"

"Sleeping Beauty's fine."

I don't know how long we were on the road after that, but I slept for part of it. It was the painful feeling of pins and needles which woke me. It was only when I saw the roof of the van that I realised I'd opened my eyes. Quickly, I tested them. I could open and close them at will. My body still felt heavy and like I was wrapped in a million layers of clothes but I wasn't completely numb. A green glow from the front of the van lit up the interior like the inside of a traffic light, giving me plenty of light to see by. Concentrating hard on my hand, I found I could move my fingers. They felt fat and cooperated as well as a softball mitt but it was better than nothing. I could tilt my head a little and I looked over at the seats. Julius was leaning against the window with a pillow between his shoulder and the side of the van. From my angle I could see into the front. Viola's long hair flowed from the seat on the left. So, Edward was now driving.

Carefully, I inched my hand to my jacket pocket. Thankfully, my left side was closest to the rear of the van and my phone hadn't fallen out or been removed. One-handed, I fumbled to pull it out and turned it on. I nearly swore out loud as I realised any messages would now sing out their presence and if I'd been missing for a few hours there was going to be plenty of messages. Hurriedly, I pushed it into my side, hoping to muffle the sound. My breath came out in a rush when I felt my phone vibrate instead. I'd had it on silent. Squinting, I revealed the glow of the screen and only saw one message from Kate and no phone calls.

Confused, I checked her message.

Thanks for letting us know about the photography conference. Late notice is better than no notice at all. I'll let Clancy know. Have fun.

That made no sense.

"At last."

I swung back to look at Edward but he'd obviously been talking to himself. My heart raced as he changed down gears and I saw the orange glow of the recognisable petrol company. I didn't have much time. I flicked through the message to the last one I'd sent Zeph, kicking myself for not putting his name against his number. I fumbled with typing the code words to let him know what was going on.

Thx 4 psnt. Using now.

I hit send but as I tried to exit the message screen Edward drove over a speed hump and my phone dropped from my hand, clattering to the floor beneath the cot I'd been strapped to. Relaxing my hand, I let it drop and closed my eyes again when I heard Julius stretch and yawn. *"Where are we?"*

"Halfway there. Check on the girl."

"She hasn't moved."

"If I have to repeat myself one more time to you—"

Viola interrupted whatever threat Edward was going to make. *"Julius, please."*

"Sure thing, Sweetpea, since you asked so nicely."

Both the front doors opened.

"Where do you think you're going?" Edward snapped.

"Bathroom. Is that alright by you?" Viola bit back.

Obviously no love lost between the members of this team.

"Hurry up. You're driving."

The car rocked even more than usual as both doors slammed. I was surprised they didn't pop out the windscreen with the force of it.

"How are we going back here, my pet?" Keeping my breathing even, I kept as still as I could. "My, you do warm up fast don't you?"

His hand went to my chest again, only this time I couldn't hold back the gasp.

"This is different. Are you holding out on me, my little pet?"

I stayed still then felt his hand move to my breast. I struck out at him with my arms which were now free but it was as effective as hitting him with a ribbon. He captured my wrists with his gloved hand then stroked my face as I glared up at him.

"Hello." He smiled, his eyes searching my face. "You are a magnificent little fighter, aren't you?"

"Let me go."

"Shhhh…" He breathed as his fingers brushed my lips, sending chills though me. "I'm afraid I can't do that. It's sad really. I was hoping you'd fight the serum, not overcome it completely. Now I really have to put you into hibernation. Can't have you escaping before you play nasty with Edward. That wouldn't do at all."

"You're crazy."

"And you are so pretty. But we need to stop playing 'state the obvious' before those two come back and spoil the fun."

His hand went back under my shirt as his mouth came down hard on mine. He forced my lips over my teeth so I couldn't bite him and I felt cold air in my mouth. Automatically, I blocked the passage with the back of my tongue and breathed through my nose. He moved his head, making it difficult to breath with his cheek in the way. He held my nose with his gloved hand. Although he'd released my wrists to do it, the chill from his other hand was burrowing though my body, making it nearly impossible to react. Using his tongue, he pushed mine out of the way and filled my lungs with freezing air. In no time at all, I passed the point of uncomfortably cold to freezing, until my shivers faded and darkness pulled me backwards with a sweet siren song of warmth.

Chapter Fourteen

I smelt smoke and hot wax as I woke and I could feel something comfortable and soft beneath me. Obviously, I was no longer in the van. Opening my eyes I cautiously looked around. It wasn't what I was expecting. Fire was easier on my eyes than artificial or natural light but it was still bright. I was in a huge four poster canopied bed with what looked and felt like fur blankets. The drapes around the bed were white and red, and shot through with gold thread so they sparkled lightly when the air moved. My head snapped around as I heard movement to my right and I scrambled to the other side of the bed so fast I nearly fell out.

"It's okay. I won't hurt you." Viola held out her hands in a placating manner but I tensed on the words 'hurt you'. The glow didn't puff much further than her mouth. "You need to take it easy. You'll have trace amounts of Edward's tranquilisers in your body and you may have a reaction."

She'd changed from the all black bad-guy outfit she'd been wearing at the park into a blue blouse and grey slacks.

"What sort of reaction?" I cleared my throat, my voice changing from a croak to a whisper.

Viola held her finger up. "The voice is from Julius' hibernation, that'll ease in time. I'm talking about nausea, vomiting, headaches, aching joints, muscle cramps, those are Edward's gifts."

I took stock of how I felt. There was a faint trace of a headache and nausea but no more than what I'd put down to my eyes. Thinking of my eyes, I brought my hands up to my face. No sunglasses. The fire and candle light was bearable but the minute I stepped out into different light it was going to be horrendous. I suppose I could put the blame on Edward but that would wear thin after a little while.

I frowned, trying to remember when they'd discussed the hibernation and if I should know about it…or if I was supposed to be paralysed. "Hibernation?"

"Basically, we put you to sleep. Or Julius did."

"You kidnapped me."

"Well, yes, I suppose you could look at it that way."

"You ambush me, perform some sort of voodoo weird crap and I wake up in a strange bed and you *suppose* I could look at it as kidnapping. How do you think I should look at it?"

I hated that my voice pulled a yo-yo party trick when I spoke, but at least Viola seemed to want to talk and I had yet to find myself handcuffed to a heater in a dingy basement somewhere.

"We needed to talk to you."

"And an invitation for coffee was out of the question?"

Viola laughed. "At least your sense of humour is intact."

I looked down as my sleeve fell from my shoulder and noticed I was dressed in some sort of cream linen, stitched at the joins with thin leather.

"Where are my clothes?" I pulled the sleeve back up.

"They were a little worse for wear."

Damn, they had my wallet, too.

"So now we've had a chat, I'd like to go home."

"You'll need to stay with us for a little while."

"I've got friends who'll be missing me."

"We've taken care of that."

I stared at her, remembering the message from Kate. "Of course you have. Obviously, Toto, we are some distance from the corn field," I muttered as I looked down at the bed. I had to keep my wits about me as I descended into this rabbit hole of what should have only been a crazy dream. I had to trust the Angelis brothers and the rest of the gang were coming for me, but in the meantime it might be best to play the wide-eyed innocent and pretend not to know a damn thing.

"You'll understand in time. But for now, are you up for a tour?"

"What?" I pulled my focus to her again, not quite sure I'd heard what I thought I'd heard.

"Tour. You know, where I show you around the place."

"I'm not a prisoner?"

"More like an unwilling guest."

"That's supposed to make me feel better?"

"It was supposed to make you smile." I kept my expression deadpanned and she shrugged. "Or not. Come with me. Moving around will make you feel better."

Stiffening, I watched the red glow for its monster effect. Nothing happened. Slowly, I got out of the bed on the opposite side to where she stood. The dress hem fell to the ground, covering my bare feet. I'd never worn anything quite so…feminine. It made me feel like one of those olden day woman; without the corset.

Viola opened the door and I automatically winced, anticipating harsh light. The hallway was brighter but still lit with low orange lights.

"Are you okay?"

I nodded and gave her the excuse she'd already handed me on a silver platter. "Headache."

"Yes. They can be nasty. Particularly the ones Edward leaves behind."

I needed to get my sunnies back from Julius or I'd be as skittish as a cat on a hot tin roof every time someone opened a door. Except, I wasn't supposed to know that he had them. This was going to be impossible.

"So this is your room." Viola grinned. "Bathroom through there."

It wasn't a hallway. That explained the low lights. "Useful."

"And you can wear anything in there."

Frowning, I watched her pull open another door. The wardrobe was so big it was almost another room. A quick peep showed a heck of a lot of dresses. I never wore dresses.

"You're providing clothes? This is messing with my mind."

Viola laughed. "I told you, you're not a prisoner. You're a guest. We'll look after you."

This time, the door she opened flooded the room with white light and I couldn't help my reaction as my eyes exploded with pain.

"Hell." Covering my face, I turned my back.

"Nova? Are you okay?"

I jerked away from her hand on my shoulder. "Shut the door."

I heard it shut and Viola came back to me. "What's the matter?"

There was nothing for it. I would have to tell her. Now that the light was gone, I turned back to her. "I suffer from photophobia. I need my sunnies. They're prescription."

"Oh?" She was quiet for a moment. "How long have you had this?"

That was tricker. I gave a snort of laughter. "It's my life."

Hopefully it would at least sound like an answer, even if it wasn't.

"I'll see what I can do."

I felt a mumbled push against the Apath barrier of my mind as she left the room. I began to pace the carpeted floor. I hadn't wanted to give away my weakness this soon. Crossing my arms, I stood near the fire. Interestingly, although the light was bright, I could look into the flames without discomfort or pain. It would be better if I started looking for a way out of here but I'd be useless once I was in the light.

A quiet knock came at the door and the room flooded with light again. I kept my back turned until I heard the door close.

My breath hissed in sharply and I tensed when I saw Julius. "What do you want?"

"It's not what I want, pet…" He smiled as he wiggled my sunnies in his hand. "It's how badly you want these."

He'd changed clothes from the park, too. Black trousers and a white, long sleeved shirt under a red t-shirt. Although he still wore gloves on his hands, he could almost pass as normal. The frost on his skin didn't hold a glow, and from what I'd experienced of him, I already knew his ability was physical. From the long clothes and the gloves, I'd say he was an untouchable.

"And how badly do I want them?" I stepped backward when he came closer.

He kept advancing until I was backed up against the bed. When I would have fallen backwards from the impact of the wooden frame against my legs, his arm snaked out and caught me around my waist. My forearms on his chest prevented him from pulling me closer.

"We have common ground, pet. We both dislike Edward. And you are going to be a very bitter pill for him to swallow."

"Why do I dislike Edward?"

Even through clothes I shivered at the cold I felt seeping from him.

"He's the reason you're here, pet." The thumb of the hand which held my sunnies caressed my face and I jerked my head back, pushing against his chest.

Suddenly, he released me and I fell backwards onto the bed. Quickly, I scrambled to the other side. Julius continued speaking as if nothing had happened. "Alas, I can't explain it to you now. That's for others. But when it happens, you'll want to talk to me. I'll be waiting." With a casual twirl of his wrist he held out my sunnies. "Do you want them or not?"

Cautiously, I approached then quickly took them from his fingers. He dropped his hand and gave a mocking bow. "Until next time."

I slid the sunnies on as he left the room. Obviously, he was trying to gain something for himself but I couldn't decide if he was crazy or simply sleazy.

Another knock came at the door but it didn't immediately open.

"Yes?"

"It's Viola. You okay if I come in?"

"I suppose so."

"Okay, so I've got three pairs but…oh."

"Julius had them."

"Julius?"

"He just left. You would have passed him in the hall."

"Oh, right. Yes."

There was something in her tone that made me think she hadn't seen him and my heart thumped. Had he been invisible somehow? Had I given myself away?

"Are you ready for the tour now?"

"I suppose so."

Stepping out into the hall, it wasn't the light that caught me off guard this time. It was the sudden cacophony of Apath. Viola took my hand as I reeled.

"It's alright. You're not going mad. I hear them too. We all do. It's just people talking."

"I wasn't expecting a crowd." I told her then frowned as I realised I'd given myself away. I had to really pull it together. It wasn't the end of the world though. Viola knew straight away I could hear it so that was confirmation they knew I'd become a Nephilim. Making a show of it, I looked down both ends of the hall. "Hang on. Ah…what's going on? There's no one here."

"They're down there." She pointed. "But I need to explain something so you don't freak out too much. The thing is…*we can speak with our minds. It's called Apath.*"

Pulling back from her, I tried to remember how I'd reacted when it happened the first time.

"Okay…" I said slowly. "Define freaking out 'too much'…because you—"

"Apathed."

"Like telepath, okay that makes sense. I mean considering you…" I cocked my head. "Do it again."

"What would you like me to say?"

"You did it before, didn't you? At the park?"

"Yes."

"This is part of that voodoo you pulled isn't it?"

"It's not voodoo."

"You can't read my mind, can you?"

Shaking her head, she laughed. *"We can only hear what you Apath."*

I stared at her. "You're kidding right?"

"No."

"I can't do that."

"Actually you can. You need some practice."

"I think I would know if I could do something like that."

"It's a recent gift."

"What makes you think that?"

"And now we come to the heart of the matter. Come with me."

I decided Viola said 'come with me' with the same frequency Zeph said 'it's impossible'. She led me down the hallway and down two flights of stairs. So much for a simple 'down there' for the voices I heard. It made me wonder how far Apath actually travelled. Viola took me to some sort of rec room. The amount of Apath should have prepared me but I was stunned at the number of Nephilim crowded into the room. There had to be at least twenty, maybe twenty-five, of them. I recognised some of them from the photos Benaiah had shown me. Feeling a little like I'd stumbled into Professor Xavier's School for the Gifted, I followed Viola rather closely when the level of Apath dropped considerably. For all the 'tells' of their abilities that I could see, I was the one who felt like a freak as they all watched me.

"Nova, this is Lauder. He'll be able to explain everything."

My gaze snapped to him as if pulled by a string. So this was Mr Bad-News himself. I don't know what I was expecting but it certainly wasn't the man I saw in front of me. I knew he was Edward's grandfather but he didn't look more than about thirty-five. He wasn't outstanding in looks but he was pleasant looking. Brown hair, slightly grey at the temples, brown eyes, slightly long face and a stocky body. He looked more like an ex-boxer than a mad scientist. A pale glow shimmered over his entire body but it was like a net which trapped multi-coloured mist which writhed over his skin.

"Nova Quinn. It is an absolute pleasure to meet you." He seemed friendly enough as he held out his hand. The mist flared from his fingertips and I hesitated.

"Mmm, no." I told him. "I'm not shaking hands with anybody around here."

Lauder smiled. "That would be Edward's doing. I don't blame you. Take a seat."

He gestured to the empty armchair beside him. Carefully, I sat and he waved his hand in a dismissive gesture. The room emptied except for Viola, Edward, Julius, Jan, and another Nephilim I didn't know whose skin looked like armour plating.

"I'd like to begin with a question." Lauder told me.

"Okay."

"How have you been feeling recently? Have you been well?"

For a second I was confused then it clicked. The leukaemia effect. All the others Benaiah had tried to heal but couldn't.

"Um…I've had a really bad flu."

"I see. And are you over it now?"

"I'm getting there. What does that have to do with anything?"

He smiled like he was a doting father and I was his favourite child. I kept as still and silent as possible as he went on to explain Nephilim. His explanation was long winded and contained enough scientific jargon and history to earn a doctorate. I much preferred the Greek god explanation myself. There was a long silence when he finished speaking and I glanced at all of them in turn, hoping I looked like I was considering whether or not to believe him.

"This is the time someone points to a camera and tells me it's all a great joke. Right?"

"It's not a joke or a prank or a fairy tale. We're Nephilim." Lauder assured me. "Julius, if you would please."

Julius unfolded himself from his chair and stood in front of us. He twinkled like someone had poured pixie-dust over him. I wasn't sure what I was supposed to be seeing but everyone else was looking at me. Glad my eyes were hidden, I brought my hand to my mouth as I tried to figure it out. Out of habit I looked for his shadow and saw it was translucent and streaked…like light through old glass.

Ice.

Light though ice.

Slowly, I stood and circled him, hoping I displayed the right amount of awe. I hoped like heck he'd turned himself into ice and I wasn't supposed to not see him at all. Holding out my hand I jerked away as he lifted his. I touched his hand. He was cold and slick under my fingertips and couldn't feel the fabric of his glove. I relaxed a little. Definitely ice.

"Man, I bet you hate global warming." I quipped.

A ripple of laugher went around the room as I backed away and reclaimed my seat.

"So what does this have to do with me?" I kept my eyes on Julius and saw him twinkle again before taking his own seat.

"We are part of a group of Nephilim who believe our abilities shouldn't be confined to those who may have been fated to be born Nephilim. It should be a gift to everyone. Nephilim and human alike."

Okay. So that wasn't the story I knew but I let Lauder continue speaking without interrupting.

"We're experimenting with Nephilim genes, trying to assimilate human and Nephilim DNA. We haven't succeeded. Until you."

"Huh? What? Me?"

"Yes, you see normally the humans who volunteer for these trials are kept under strict supervision and everything is monitored and recorded. Unfortunately Edward here…" He gestured to him. "…took it upon himself to not only create his own gene but to inject you with it, in a public place, without observation."

"He what?"

I looked down at my hand as though I was putting two and two together.

"It wasn't static electricity." Edward told me with a faint smile.

"You…you prick."

My anger wasn't faked. I was glad to finally have the opportunity to take it out on him. I was up and out of my chair before I'd thought about it. I wanted to hit him but the sight of his quills stopped me. I wasn't sure what damage I'd do to myself if I did actually touch him.

"Yes." His smiled broadened as he looked up at me. "I am actually."

Smug bastard. Closing my eyes, I swung out. My hand connected with firm flesh and no quills. My eyes opened and he sat with his head turned to the side. Slowly, he turned back to me.

"Feel better?"

With a snarl, I lashed out with both hands. He was the reason I could no longer take photos. He'd ruined the only life I'd ever known. He was the reason for the headaches, the illness, the pain and these bloody eyes. He was the reason my human side was dying and trying to kill me in the process. I wasn't anywhere close to feeling better.

Surging to his feet, he pushed me back across the room. I stumbled but I wasn't anywhere close to finished with him yet. Fuelled with fury I ran back to him only to be pulled back by Viola's order to stop. I was pinned to the spot as though tied down by guy-ropes. Struggling against the red glow as it trapped me, I heard Edward's laughter.

"Having a little problem there?"

Screaming in frustration, I sent an Apath to the red glow.

"Let me go."

Like last time it worked and I could see Edward's shock as I closed the gap between us and grabbed his hand. Slamming it to his chest I directed an Apath to his quills.

"Paralysis serum. Human DNA."

He flinched twice, then dropped like a stone.

Suddenly I felt steel bands wrap around me. I struggled against them but they tightened so much they were crushing me. I very nearly couldn't breathe.

"Settle down. Shhhh. It's okay. Calm down now."

The voice was soft and soothing in my ear. It was at complete odds to the amour-like arms which wrapped around me. Like a deluge, the anger left my body and I slumped in the Nephilim's embrace, hating the fact that I'd been so angry, I was now crying.

"Well, that was exciting." Lauder mused, crossing over to me and gently moving my hair off my face. He peered at me as he lifted my chin when I started shaking. "I think you're in shock now, aren't you?"

"She's in shock?" Viola's voice came out high pitched. "Am I the only one who noticed that she completely disregarded my direct order?"

Jan checked Edward's pulse. "He'll live."

"Pity." Julius sighed from behind me.

"Julius." Viola frowned.

"What, Sweetpea? I only said what everyone else was thinking."

"Can you tell me what you did?" Lauder asked gently.

My breath hitched as I shook my head and whispered. "I don't know. I don't know."

I couldn't really make sense of it. I was so angry, I reacted. I didn't think it through. I wasn't sure what I'd done. I wasn't sure how. It happened so fast.

"One thing is for certain." Lauder wrapped his hand around the nape of my neck and I felt warmth flood though me, defusing all the tension in my neck, shoulders and all the way down my back. "You're one of us. You're a Nephilim."

Dropping my head, I stared at the swirling pattern on the carpet. I might now be Nephilim…but there was no way in hell I was one of them.

Chapter Fifteen

With a sigh, I slid the next one along, and the next and the next. I knew that compared to going naked I shouldn't complain, but really, they could have provided something other than dresses. The one I wore was alright but I'd worn it for nearly two days straight. Pausing, I heard a knock on the door and ignored it. I didn't want anything to do with anyone at the moment. I looked at the next one, then the next one after that. Granted, they were pretty dresses, but pretty dresses were still dresses. My searching stilled as I felt a cold wash of air behind me.

"The Ice Man cometh." I sighed as I turned around. Not surprisingly, Julius stood there. I tried to cover my apprehension with a show of annoyance. "An unanswered knock usually means you're not invited in."

"It could also mean the chicken has flown the coop."

"Empty or not, no fox is welcome in the hen house."

"Pretty and witty. You're not gay are you?"

I blinked at him, surprised he knew West Side Story. "That's not the subtext."

"You've got to give me points for trying."

"Points given. You are very trying." I pushed past him.

"You surprised me last night, little pet."

"I'm not your pet." I snapped. I was sick and tired of him calling me that. "And I want you out of this room."

"Yes, well we can't all have what we want. Poor Edward though. I knew you'd be a bitter pill for him to swallow."

"Alright. You've had your gloat. Now you may leave."

"I'm sensing slight hostility."

"Slight? You froze me three times."

"Yes, well, Edward gave you three shots of paralysis serum."

"So you thought you'd even the score?"

"I thought I would protect you from the side effects. Edward's tranquilisers trample your nerves, sweetheart. By freezing them I sent them to sleep so they didn't feel battered and bruised when they kicked back into gear. I'm pretty sure I judged it right. You didn't have a single ill effect, did you?"

I didn't like that he was right so I went on the offensive. "So now you're the good guy."

Julius laughed. "I wouldn't go that far, Sweetheart."

"Don't call me that."

"You said not to call you pet, now you don't want sweetheart. What should I call you?"

"How about you don't call me anything? Don't talk to me. Don't Apath…or whatever it is. Don't anything. Just walk out that door and pretend I don't exist."

"No, I don't think I will."

Frustrated, I turned on my heel, went into the bathroom and locked the door behind me. Gripping the edge of the sink, I glared down the plughole. I knew I couldn't stay in here forever, but I hoped that by the time I'd finished, Julius would have gotten bored and left. I went to push away from the sink when something strange in the mirror brought my attention back to my reflection. I hadn't looked into a mirror since Tiberius imaged my eyes. The black irises were too disconcerting. Lifting my hand, I passed my fingers through the faint glow around my head. It was a deep red colour. So deep it was burgundy burgeoning on black. So far I had yet to see this colour red on anyone else. It was level with my eyes and appeared to ring my head like an ill-fitting halo. Removing my glasses, I saw the glow either went into or came from my eyes, and that the black irises had changed colour to match it. My eyes might have been the same colour but under the halo they didn't actually glow.

"Physical…" I breathed on shaky breath. "…with non-physical elements, maybe? Red is control. Control of what?"

I sank down to the edge of the bathtub before I fell down. I hadn't even thought that I'd be able to see my own ability. Obviously there was something more than simply seeing things. I started counting back the days. I didn't know exactly how many days I'd been here but the day in the park had been four weeks after Aiden's birthday. Two weeks before that I'd seen Edward for the proofs. Another two weeks or so before that I'd met Ransom for the first time; three, maybe four days after Edward…it was close enough to two months, maybe a touch more. One of the brothers, I couldn't remember which one now, told me that pitch eyes disappeared two-to-four months after birth. Having the ability show up as a visual now made sense. Only, I didn't know what it meant exactly.

I looked down at my hands. Control? What control did I have?

Suddenly, I remembered Viola's red glow. I'd ordered it away from me, not once but twice. Stunned, I lifted my head and stared at the white wall glowing orange under the coloured light. I'd also used Edward's quills on him, simply by Apathing what I wanted to have injected into him.

That's it. That's what I had done. I had direct Apathed their abilities. I hadn't even been aware I could do that. I did it. Just like breathing. Zeph was right.

Who knew Edward had human DNA hidden in his quills? But he must have. He'd flinched twice. If the human DNA messed with his Nephilim DNA the same way mine did, then his punishment fit the crime. In my books at least.

I wanted to test out this theory further. I grinned as I turned toward the bedroom door. And I knew the perfect guinea pig.

*****

I wanted to be in a crowd so that Julius wouldn't immediately know it was me…if it worked. But there was a second problem I hadn't counted on. Indirect Apath, though mostly mumbled, could still be listened to. As much as I wanted to mess with him, I wanted to be able to do it in a way that no could tell what I was doing.

"What are you doing in here all alone? And in the dark?"

"Reading."

"Well, a library is the place to do so." I didn't look up as Lauder claimed the seat across from me. *"Are you certain you don't want more light?"*

"The candle's fine."

"You don't have to hide yourself away. No one will hurt you."

"Yeah, but I could hurt them."

He reached across and laid his hand on mine. His colours started dancing over my skin and I pulled my hand away. "Don't beat yourself up over Edward, Nova. He'll be fine."

"Fine? So the talk I've heard about him being sick from the moment he woke up is someone's idea of a joke?"

He didn't answer but his silence spoke volumes. I think my guilt-ridden act worked.

"What are you reading?"

I closed the book over my finger to read the title. "Apath. The concept and actualisation."

"Practice helps you understand it better than reading about it."

"Yeah, Viola's way ahead of you in voicing that theory. It's just that..."

"Just that…?"

"Well, sometimes I can hear the voices in my head clearly and sometimes it's like I'm hearing it from another room." I tapped the book. "I get, now, that there are two ways to Apath but I was trying to find a way to stop the mumbles. It makes me feel like people are whispering about me and I'd rather not hear it."

"Firstly, and I say this with my tongue firmly planted, not all conversations are about you—"

I smiled. "I know, but it's like someone speaking a foreign language in front of you. They could be saying 'hello, how are you', but it makes you feel like an outsider whether they mean to or not."

Lauder nodded. "Unfortunately, you're out of luck. Direct Apath to another person will always be whispers."

Placing my chin in my hand, I looked across at him for a moment. "To another person? Does that mean you can direct Apath to animals and not have it happen?"

Obviously, Lauder found that extremely funny. "No one can Apath to animals…or plants, before you ask, it doesn't work that way."

"I thought Apath was like spoken conversation?"

"Alright, let me rephrase. You can Apath to, like you can talk to, animals and plants, but there is not going to be a return Apath. If your ability allows you to communicate to animals or plants…fine, but it's not Apath."

"There are people who can communicate with animals and plants?"

"Nephilim abilities are as varied as the person themselves."

I saw my chance. "So what's your ability?"

"I can affect what people feel."

"Feel? Like emotions?"

He shook his head. "Physically. The other night with Edward, do you remember afterwards when Felix held you, how did you feel?"

"I don't know, there was too much –."

"Do you remember a moment when you felt like you'd had a relaxing back massage?"

I made my eyes widen in what I hoped looked like surprise. "That was you?"

"Yes."

"So you can…heal?"

"Nothing so noble I'm afraid, although I wish I could. I deal more with the symptoms than the disease. If I'd been there when you'd had your flu, I could have made the aches and pains fade away but I wouldn't have been able to do anything for the fever or boost your energy levels."

Benaiah could heal, Lauder was one giant painkiller, but they both had rainbows…in a manner of speaking. Rainbows could mean an ability which dealt with the human body. However, unlike Benaiah, Lauder wore short sleeved shirts and touched whoever he wanted.

"That's still a cool power."

"Ability, Nova. We don't call them powers."

"So can I do that too?"

"As I said before, abilities are as varied as the person themselves. Your ability will be unique to you."

"But I do have one?"

"Judging by what you did to Edward, it's a given. We need to figure out what it is and how to control it."

"Yeah, you wouldn't want more of your gang getting sick."

Lauder laughed softly. "There is always a little havoc when abilities first emerge. You can't learn to walk without falling down some."

Chapter Sixteen

I was surprised that I pretty much had free rein. I could go anywhere I pleased. Even outside, though there were never less than ten or so Nephilim around except when I went to my room. That was the only place I had privacy…if I didn't count Julius' constant visits, that was. He was infuriating. The rest of the Nephilim seemed friendly enough. I could have been on some sort of retreat. Viola had even found me a point and shoot camera.

It was weird that there wasn't much technology anywhere. No phones, no TV, no computers, no internet. The library was wall-to-wall books and an old catalogue card system. There was a microwave in the kitchen and a projector for movies and a few game consoles but nothing with information. I couldn't find a clock or calendar anywhere.

I took photos of the Nephilim then spent hours studying the 'tells' I saw. None of them had a problem with showing off their abilities in front of me and I walked around pretending to be like a kid in a candy store. Soooo enamoured of their wonderful and mighty abilities when little ol' me was still trying to figure out my own.

I even agreed to their testing to see if anything triggered my apparent latent abilities, then I let them run around like chickens with their head cut off while they tried to figure out what the results meant. In the meantime, I kept practicing and trying to mess up the results in the first place.

"Can we…stop…please?"

I was exhausted and my muscles screamed at me but my body kept running on the treadmill.

"You're not even trying."

Gritting my teeth, I gripped the bar in front of me and with willpower tried to slow my legs. It was trying to fight gravity. I managed to stop moving for a split second but it was more like a pause between steps. Slumping, I gave up. My body should have fallen but it went back to running.

"I can't do it."

"You can. You've done it before."

"Let her go, Viola."

I kept running for a moment longer before Viola obeyed Lauder's quietly spoken order. She released me so fast I stumbled then fell, the treadmill taking me backwards and depositing me in a legless heap on the floor.

"Viola!" Lauder snapped.

"Oh my gosh, I'm so sorry."

I felt a hand on my shoulder and the agony from my muscles and ache in my chest melted away.

"Can you stand?" Lauder asked near my ear.

"Give me a minute." Despite no longer having any pain, I felt weak and shaky.

"How long have you been at this?"

"I don't know."

"Viola?"

"A little while."

"That's not an answer."

"Alright, two hours. But she can…"

"How dare you?" Lauder's hand left my back and moved away from me.

"You don't understand. She can do it. She can break my command."

"I don't care if she can shoot fireballs from her eyes, you do not give level sixteen training to a child."

"She's not a child."

"Leave now."

I'd never heard an Apath so angry. The volume level hadn't changed but the fury was palpable.

"I told her she could." I Apathed.

Lauder returned to my side and supported me as I tried to sit up. "Five minutes would have been enough to know that you couldn't break free."

"I did before. At least she thinks I did. When I was angry at Edward."

"When abilities manifest it's usually high emotions that gets them started. A temper tantrum isn't an unusual trigger."

Shaking badly, I went to the chair and almost fell into it. "You really do think I'm a child don't you?"

He sank down on his hunches in front of me, brushing my sweaty hair from my face. "I'm referring to your abilities. Your abilities are in the infant stage. We need to draw them out as we would for a child.

We can't treat you like an adult who has been familiar with their abilities for years."

"Okay, I guess that makes sense."

"You don't believe me do you?" He asked softly.

I swallowed hard. There was something intense in his eyes and I was magnetized.

"I believe you." I whispered. My heart beat went up a notch and I could feel a tingle of anticipation as he eyes dropped to my mouth. My breathing was loud in my ears as he leaned closer. His lips were warm, soft yet hard. Of their own accord my eyes closed and I lifted my chin. His kiss was the most amazing thing I'd ever felt. It was as if the most mouth-watering, lightest, sweetest piece of chocolate had melted on my tongue, leaving me yearning for more. This time the shiver that went through me had nothing to do with exhaustion.

When he pulled away I moaned, hating the emptiness I felt. Slowly, I opened my eyes to see him smiling softly at me.

"There is nothing child-like about you." He whispered.

Lifting my hand I placed it at his neck to bring him closer. I didn't want him to stop kissing me. The sight of his rainbow running over my skin and straight down my arm made me suddenly realise that while my body wanted this to continue, my mind was screaming warning sirens at me. There was something dangerously wrong with this situation.

Dropping my head, I forced a strangled laugh then fought to bring my hand down from his shoulder. "I think…I'm more tired than I realise."

Flooding heat coursed through me, leaving behind a coil of desire and I gasped. Lauder seemed to take that as an invitation because he brought his lips to mine again. I couldn't help lifting my hand and kissing him back. Even as I did, my mind rebelled and anger coursed through me. Allowing my eyes to close again, I focused on my anger as he pulled me closer to him. Despite my anger, I didn't want him to know what I could do.

Seeing his rainbow in my mind, I pushed the thought of it lifting a tissue-paper thin distance from my body through the chilled-honey barrier. Desire drained from me leaving me feeling dirty and violated. Opening my eyes I brought my hands against his chest and pushed hard.

"No."

I could see the stunned look on his face. Pushing again, I stood at the same time, breaking free of his hold. I didn't give him a chance to touch me again as I ran from the gymnasium. I didn't stop until I reached my room. The damn door didn't have a lock. Crawling onto the bed, I tossed my glasses on the bedside table and buried myself under the blankets. As a child it had worked to keep the boogie man from getting me. For a while after Aiden's death I'd done it, trying to hide from the world. It wouldn't do much to protect me here, but there was a comfort to it as I curled in the almost complete darkness. It wasn't fair. I had three blankets over me and I could still see. Just.

Lauder could control more than pain and I almost fell for it. By pushing him away, I may have allowed him to figure out my ability. It was obvious that being able to resist him had been unusual. With a shuddering sigh, I hugged the pillow to my middle as I was overwhelmed with hopelessness. For the first time since Aiden's death I was totally and utterly alone.

"Nova? Are you alright?"

I stiffened. "Go away."

"Come on, pet, talk to me."

"I don't want to talk to you. Go. Away."

"It's obvious you're upset."

"You think?" I snapped sarcastically.

"What's the matter?"

"The matter?" I flung my hands out, pushing the covers from over my head. From the way Julius jerked back I think I nearly hit him in the process. "I don't know. What could possibly be the matter? I'm a freak. I've been taken from everyone I know, everyone I love."

To my shock, I burst into tears. Bringing the covers back up, I buried myself again.

I felt a gentle weight and from the cool seeping through the blankets, I figured he was stroking me. I jerked up again and swung out with the pillow, knocking him onto the floor.

"Don't touch me. I've had enough of people touching me today." I glared at him.

He calmly looked up at me from the floor and his calm pissed me off. I threw the pillow with all my might. He ducked as it hit him with a *wumph* then bounced harmlessly off his forearm.

It didn't make me feel any better. I buried myself again. "Go away."

There was silence for a few moments then I heard him move. He didn't say anything and I relaxed, figuring he'd left. A few seconds later a firm *wumph* hit my side. I flung the covers back.

"You did not just do that."

I saw the pillow in his hands. Damn ogre. He'd hit me with it. Reaching up, I grabbed the second pillow and swung out. He danced back then leaned in, hitting me with his pillow. It was on for young and old, trading pillow whacks like children. I wanted to stay mad at him, but I couldn't. In fits of laughter I collapsed against the bed, nearly unable to move. Running two hours today followed by this little stint had about done me in.

Julius sank down beside me, setting the pillow vertically behind him. I hugged mine despite the wooden edge of the bed digging into my shoulders.

"Feel better?"

"No." Catching his glance I smiled. "Maybe."

"What happened?"

"You're really nosy, you know that don't you?"

"No, actually I don't."

Resting my chin on the top of the pillow, I drew up my knees and stared at the fire.

"Do you have a fire in your room, too?"

He tilted his head. "I have a fire place."

"You melt?"

Julius huffed a breath. "I don't mind the cold."

I continued watching the dancing flames until an idea came to me. He obviously wanted me to confide in him, Edward thought I had a boyfriend and Lauder would need a plausible explanation as to why I'd been able to resist him. I wasn't someone who usually told lies, but it wasn't a lie. Really. Much.

"Have you ever loved someone, Julius?"

"As in…?"

"A girl?"

"Not really."

"If you did, do you think you would forgive her for kissing someone else?"

He stilled beside me and slowly turned his head. "I'm not sure. I suppose it would depend on the situation."

"I kissed Lauder today. Well, he kissed me, but then I kissed him back. I shouldn't have done it. I know that. The worst part was that I didn't want to stop."

"But you did stop?" I nodded into the pillow and he shifted beside me. "How?"

"What do you mean, how?"

"I mean…well, you know what I mean. If you didn't want to stop, why did you?"

I smiled into the fabric. Julius obviously knew what Lauder could do.

"Seriously? You're asking me that?"

He shrugged. "It's not against the law to kiss a guy, pet."

"A guy who appears to be the ring leader for a group of Nephilim who kidnapped me?"

"Well, when you put it like that." He teased.

I sighed again, hoping I wasn't laying it on too thick. "He made me feel…I don't know…like the rest of the world didn't exist. But it does exist and part of that world is my boyfriend, and I've got no business kissing other guys, no matter how they make me feel or how much I miss him."

Out of the corner of my eye I saw the smile slowly curve Julius' mouth before he hurriedly smoothed his features. "You managed to resist Lauder because you felt guilty kissing him, when you have a boyfriend?"

"Uh huh."

His smiled twitched again, but he managed to control himself. "Well, pet, don't beat yourself up over it. You faced temptation and you won."

I turned my head to face him. "I did, didn't I?"

"Feel better now?"

"I suppose so. Julius?"

"Yes, pet?"

"Will you please go away now?"

Chuckling, he rose to his feet. "Since you asked so nicely."

Staying where I was, I watched him leave the room, then smiled into the pillow. "And will you pretty please tell Lauder what I just told you."

Chapter Seventeen

Glancing up from my book, I saw Lauder across the room surrounded by his tag team. I had kept my distance from him. If I had to be near him I mimicked Benaiah's mannerisms and didn't let him touch me. Hopefully, he would think I was painfully embarrassed. In the meantime, I was fairly confident I had figured out everyone's abilities, at least enough of what they could do so I could deflect them if needed.

Hiding in my wardrobe was a pillow case with food and water, tied with two belts fashioned to work like backpack straps. All I had to do now was to figure out where the hell I was and which direction I needed to go.

I looked back down at the picture of the southern sky in the book of astronomy. I really needed a GPS. I needed my phone. Pity my phone was in the back of a van somewhere and I hadn't seen a single vehicle since I got here. Besides, by now it would have run out of battery. But Edward had a phone.

Come to think of it, I hadn't actually seen Edward since the time I'd zapped him with his own quills.

Rising from the couch, I went over to where Felix was pouring himself a cup of coffee.

"Felix, where's Edward?"

"You're supposed to be practicing Apath, remember?"

"Where's Edward?"

"You want to kick his butt some more?"

"I haven't seen him for a while. I know Lauder says he's fine, but I haven't...you know, seen him with my own eyes to be sure."

"I saw him yesterday. He's fine."

So much for that idea. I didn't want to push it further in case he became suspicious.

"Want to play table tennis?" He asked, talking a mouthful of the coffee.

I gave him a smile. *"Do I want to get thrashed, you mean?"*

He shrugged. *"Whatever floats your boat."*

"I think I'll pass. Besides, I can't really move that well in these long skirts. What do I have to do around here to get some trousers?"

"Pass novice stage on your training." I wasn't sure if it was a quip or not but my scowl seemed to make him happy.

"I think I'll go for a walk. That, at least, I can do in a long skirt."

"Suit yourself. I'm going to see if Gus wants to lose some more money."

I watched him go. Felix and Augustus. The team no one wanted to play. They both blatantly cheated then vehemently denied it. Kind of like Zeph.

Blinking back the tears, I stared at the tower of cardboard cups. I needed to get out of here. I'm pretty sure I had held it together so far but I was only one person and I wasn't used to this subterfuge. I was no Jason Bourne. Heck, even he had Marie. All I had was a book on the stars.

Hugging the book to my chest, I walked through the mansion to the back yard. A yard might have been a touch of an understatement. It had a yard like Pemberley had a yard. About six or seven hundred metres from the back courtyard was the start of a hedge maze. By now I had it memorised and found the grassed centre. Lying on my back, I rested the book on my tummy and looked up at the stars. I'd taken to the habit a few nights ago. No Nephilim bothered me here. No one walked passed every seven minutes. I smiled as I saw the green light whizz across my view of the night sky. I'd figured green meant tracking. Not checking on me didn't mean they didn't keep tabs on me.

I pushed my sunnies to the top of my head and looked down at the page in the book before looking back up. I was pretty sure they matched. At least close enough. So I had approximate longitude and latitude, but I didn't have a map. My hope now was that I could somehow get the coordinates to Zeph, find a place close by to hide then wait for him to pick me up. I wasn't stupid. As far as plans went it was pretty flimsy. A close enough match could be miles and miles out. I could be putting us both in danger. Hearing footsteps, I lowered the book again. Whoever it was stopped close by but I could feel the wash of cold air.

"Do you not understand the concept of privacy?"

"Vaguely."

"So what's this? You finish the pow-wow with the boss man and want to make sure the good little kidnap victim is behaving herself?"

"If you want to look at it that way." Julius told me as he lay down on the grass.

Even though he'd positioned himself so he lay to the opposite point of the compass to me, his head was near my shoulder and I shivered.

"You're cold." I told him.

"I know."

"Do you ever wish you were normal?"

"I'm Nephilim. I don't think there is a normal."

"Good point."

"You a fan of star gazing?" He asked casually.

"Not normally. But I am a fan of privacy."

"Is that a hint?"

"Do you need a broader one?"

"If you want to give me one, I'm happy to ignore either."

"So, are you following orders or are you a self-appointed babysitter?"

"I don't need an excuse to spend time with you but it helps."

"So how come they didn't appoint Viola, it would make more sense."

"Pecking order."

I turned slightly so I could see him out of the corner of my eye. "Are you being punished for something?"

His laughter rang out. "No, pet, I'm not being punished."

A green light whizzed over again. So even with a babysitter they still kept tabs on me.

"How old were you when you found out you had powers?"

"Abilities." He corrected.

"Whatever."

"Don't know. I guess it's a little like walking. At some stage you had to have learned, and you know children are taught but you don't actually remember being taught."

I felt tugging at my scalp and frowned. "Are you playing with my hair?"

"It was lying there."

I had pulled my braid out flat behind me so it wasn't uncomfortable beneath me. Lifting my head, I ran my hand down and tugged it out of his grasp, letting it fall over my shoulder. "Well don't."

"Why not?"

"What do you mean, why not?"

"Why don't you want me to play with your hair?"

"You're kidding right?"

"No."

"We are not girls at a slumber party, you do not get to play with my hair. It's not a toy…besides you'll freeze it."

Julius blew a raspberry. "Give me a little credit. I don't often see hair as long as yours."

"Aiden liked it long."

I winced as soon as the words were out of my mouth. I really had to watch what I said.

"Aiden? Your boyfriend?"

"Aiden, none of your damn business."

He made a sound like a bomb exploding. "Shot down in flames."

"So where are you in the pecking order?" I asked
to change the subject.

"Higher than some, lower than others."

"Lower than Viola?"

"You already know that."

"Lower than Edward?"

Julius snorted. "He wishes."

"It sounded like he was giving the orders on my
kidnapping."

"Edward is a nobody related to a somebody, so by
default has been placed in a position of something
when by his own merit he would have never even
reached the first rung of nothing."

I could hear the bitterness in his tone.

"So why did this nothing-something decide to take
it upon himself to inject a random human…and why
did it have to be me?"

"That's something you'll have to ask him."

"I would. Except, I'm not so sure there isn't a
manslaughter suit somewhere with my name on it."

"You didn't kill him, pet."

"Are you sure? I haven't seen him around."

I heard the grass crinkle and Julius shifted until he
was on his forearms looking across at me. "I don't
know what you did, but it is messing with him. His
abilities aren't working like they used to and he's
struggling with Apath. He's confined to the infirmary
because there is no guarantee that he can control what
he does. I think it's wonderful, pet, but he's not
dead."

Leaning on one arm, he tapped my nose. I scowled
at him but he took no notice as he settled himself on
his back again.

After a moment, I pressed my luck. "I take it you're not on speaking terms with him?"

"By choice."

"Does the infirmary have visiting hours?"

He rolled onto his arms again and studied me for a minute or two. "You really do want to speak with him?"

"Nephilim don't have a 'normal', Julius, but humans do. And he took that away from me, so yes, I want to talk to him."

*****

About two days later I felt a gentle tug on my braid as I pretended to attempt solving a coloured puzzle with touch alone.

"Stop it, Julius." I muttered.

"Apath Nova." Viola chided.

Sighing, I pulled the blindfold from my face then shielded my eyes until I could put my sunnies on.

"Sorry. He's completely ruined my concentration."

"Well, you might not have solved the puzzle, but you knew it was Julius behind you."

"Yeah, the multiplying chills were in no way a clue."

"At least you didn't lose control." He quipped as he dropped onto the beanbag beside us.

"She's not going to grow comfortable with Apath if you don't encourage it." Viola glared at him.

"Sorry, sweetpea."

"Why would she lose control?"

Julius pointed in my direction. *"I was adding to her quote."*

"You quoted something?"

"Grease. Paraphrased." I could tell Viola was completely confused.

"You need an education, sweetpea."

"Well, excuse me if I spent my education learning more important things." She snapped. *"We will continue later."*

"What stick is up her butt this time?" Julius asked as Viola stormed away.

"I think she's disappointed she doesn't know the musical…" I watched his smile. "…or it could be that I couldn't solve the puzzle."

"I can't solve that puzzle with a blindfold either."

"Yes, but you at least know what your ability is."

He swiped a chip from the packet on the table. "A puzzle isn't going to reveal yours either."

"You sound so sure."

He shrugged. "You didn't need a puzzle to take Edward down. Speaking of which, I got you an appointment."

"You did? When?"

Looking at his wrist he pretended to consult a watch which wasn't there. "About now. Interested?"

I scrambled to my feet only to trip over the hem of the skirt. Julius grabbed my upper arms as I tripped, his strength the only thing keeping us from colliding. I steadied myself and pushed away.

"Sorry."

"A simple thank you would have sufficed."

I clipped the back of his head with a quick swipe. He laughed and clambered to his feet but I almost had heart failure. Aiden had been the last person I'd done that to.

"You going to finish these chips?"

"They're Viola's."

"In that case…" Julius collected the packet before leading the way.

I was glad I had a guide. I would never have known where to go and I didn't think I'd remember the way. Perhaps that was the point.

Edward looked…in a word, awful. He was gaunt with black rings under his eyes. His hair was all over the place and he sported a messy beard. He had a grey t-shirt on and blankets up to his hips. I could see bruises on his arms and he was hooked up to oxygen and a drip. It was hard looking at him. In the comfort of my own anger I had thought this was a fitting punishment but I wasn't a complete monster.

"Have you come to gloat?" His voice held a rough and breathless quality.

"I did. She came for answers."

I frowned. "Julius, that was uncalled for."

He looked offended. "It's the truth."

"Can you wait outside?"

"Nope."

"Can you at least stand over there and keep your mouth shut?"

"No promises." He shrugged as he went and leaned against the wall.

Spying a chair, I dragged it over to the side of the bed. Now that I was here I didn't know where to start. "I guess I want to know why."

"Because Y's a crooked letter and Zed's no better."

"Edward, please?"

"I guess we're even now, so it shouldn't really matter."

"If you hadn't done it to me I wouldn't have been able to do it to you." I pointed out.

"Yeah, Karma's a real bitch. I get that. Thank you."

"I want to understand—"

"Why did I create the gene in the first place?" He shrugged. "To prove that I can. To prove that I'm not the dumb fu—"

"Edward." Julius growled from the corner.

Edward turned his head to look at him with tired distain before turning back to me. "Dumb idiot…" He amended. "…that everyone thinks I am. To prove that I knew where Lauder was going wrong, even if he didn't believe me. As for giving the gene to you…well, I can't really answer that."

"Try."

"I didn't choose you, I didn't pick you, I didn't even pull your name out of a hat. You were sitting there on your own and I wanted to see if I could chat you up. End of story. It was supposed to be a bit of fun while I waited for ice cream."

"So what changed your mind?"

"Nothing. I didn't change my mind. I shook your hand and for the first time in my life, I triggered without meaning to."

Julius snorted. "That's not what your last girlfriend told me."

I saw Edward's jaw clench as he glared at Julius. I placed my hand on his and he brought his attention back to me. For a moment he looked down at my hand then slowly moved his hand under mine to hold it. I wasn't comfortable with him holding my hand, but his hold was weak and there was something in his expression that kept me still. He dropped his cocky attitude and I could see frightened uncertainty.

"The gene was for me and that is the honest truth."

"For you?"

"Lauder keeps injecting humans with his version of the gene trying to create Nephilim. I'm seven-eighths human. It should have worked."

Suddenly, he gripped my hand hard. It felt like my hand broke. Edward's back arched. His scream of pain was terrifying.

Julius moved fast. Tearing off his glove, he shoved Edward's shirt up and placed his hand on his chest at the same time as he gripped his nose and placed his mouth over Edward's like he was giving him CPR.

After a few seconds Edward slumped back down and Julius moved away. The heart monitor which had been spiking all over the place suddenly pulled into a straight line as Julius removed my hand from Edward's.

"You killed him."

"No, pet. Hibernation."

After a long drawn out pause, one single blip bounced on the screen and I let out a sigh of relief. Three people in white suddenly rushed into the room and Julius quickly explained. They took his explanation in stride and bustled us out of the room.

"Give me your hand." Julius told me the second we were out in the hallway.

I could barely move it. The pain was making me nauseous.

"Hold on, pet, this'll be better than a cold compress."

He removed the second glove and cupped my hand top and bottom. My hand went from painful to cold to numb. The nausea faded and I took a few breaths to steady myself.

"Did it feel like he pricked you at all?"

"No. I don't think so."

Biting my lip, I looked back through the window of the door of Edward's room. I could see him despite the medical staff. I didn't think he would ever be capable of pricking anyone again.

His quills had disappeared.

Chapter Eighteen

Something wasn't right. Opening my eyes, I saw a figure crouching at the side of the bed. I reared back even as I felt the cold air and saw it was Julius.

"Shhh, shhh, pet, shhh. I'm getting you out of here."

"What?"

"We don't have long, but you have to trust me."

"Why the hell should I trust you?" I frowned as I stared at the contraption on his face.

"Look…"

"Don't 'look' me." I snapped.

His head swung around to the door. "Quiet."

I followed his gaze and the door remained shut.

"What?" I hissed, dropping my voice.

"Lauder got the test results back for Edward today and now he's kicked everything up a gear. Here, change into these. Quickly." Taking my hand, he pressed fabric into it.

"What are they?"

"Jeans, shirt and a jacket. I've got boots here, too. Hurry."

"Not until you tell me what's going on."

"Short version is that Lauder doesn't want to share Nephilim abilities, he's trying to isolate the Angel gene and he is using humans as guinea pigs. Nephilim can't breed with Nephilim. He hopes that a created Nephilim can and that the child will have a stronger Angel gene."

That, at least, was a lot closer to the story the Angelis brothers had told me.

"So what does Edward have to do with it?

"While you dress."

Flipping the covers back, I swung my legs out of bed and began pulling on the jeans under the long night dress I wore.

"Whatever you did the other week —"

"Week? How long have I been here?"

"Nine weeks—"

"Nine weeks?"

"We really don't have time for this." Julius hissed.

Jumping into the jeans I did the clasp as I went to the dresser for a bra. Pulling my arms in I began putting it on under the top of the dress.

"Keep talking." I glanced up at him and saw him focused on me. "And turn around."

He smiled. "It's dark, Nova."

"You've got night vision goggles on, so turn the hell around."

"You can see in the dark?"

Mentally, I kicked myself. I hadn't meant to let that be known. "I thought we didn't have time for this."

"Edward is human." Julius said as he turned.

I froze. "What?"

"You turned him human. It's quite ironic actually. The one guy who wanted to be more Nephilim than the one-eighth he is and you've turned him completely human. Lauder thinks if you can turn a Nephilim into a human in a few short weeks, you can turn a human into a Nephilim."

"And if I can, he wants to breed them."

"He wants to breed with you."

A shiver of disgust ran though me. I lifted the dress over my head and pulled on the shirt as I sat on the bed, then grabbed the boots.

"So why should I trust you?"

Julius turned without my permission but as I was lacing a boot it didn't matter. "Pet, I promise I will tell my entire life story, but when we are far, far away from here."

"Don't call me pet."

"Look, Nova –."

"And don't 'look' me either. I hate it."

He hitched a grin. "Worse than pet?"

"Why should I trust you?" I repeated, glaring at him.

"There are plenty of humans out there who are willing to give away their humanity for cash and the promise of Nephilim ability. Use them up, spit them out, I don't care. They consented. You didn't. Trust me or don't trust me, it's up to you. But whatever your choice is, make it quick."

Dropping my foot to the floor, I stared at the door as a red glow seeped through it. "I think we just ran out of time."

I hadn't realised Viola could control through walls, but as the sound of footsteps came down the hallway,

Julius grabbed my jacket, hooked an arm around my waist and hauled me to my feet.

"Keep as still as possible. They won't see you unless you move." He breathed into my ear.

I saw the pixie-dust twinkle descend over the both of us and as it danced in a light mist over my shirt sleeve I figured he'd turned us both to ice. It was hard to keep still when I was pressed against a man who felt like an ice block but I wasn't about to move.

The red glow seeped into the room. It looked hesitant, searching. Breathing in slowly, I focused on it and fed it the thought that it couldn't feel, find or sense us.

"Hell."

"Nova…" He hissed as he fought me when I strained against his arm.

"Glasses."

He loosened his hold. Grabbing them I stepped back into his arms and he iced me again as the door opened. I could feel his heart pound against my hand. For some absurd reason there was something amusing about the fact Mr Ice-Man himself wasn't as chilled as he made out.

"What the hell…?"

Viola's voice was loud as a bright light flooded the room. My eyes slammed shut as Julius winced. With the night vision goggles he wouldn't have fared any better than I did. I can not tell you how nerve wracking it is to stand against the wall of a room, knowing you would normally be in plain sight, unable to see if the other person could see you or not and trying not to move in an effort to remain invisible.

Needless to say, it wasn't only Julius' heartbeat which raced.

From the way the light moved, I figured Viola held a torch of some kind. I heard the blankets being shoved aside, followed by the slamming open of the bathroom door. I could feel the movement of air brushing past as Viola inspected the wardrobe then a second time when she went to the window, pulling aside the curtains with a screech of metal rings on the curtain rods.

"Full alert. All units spread out. Baby is missing."

The light disappeared but neither of us moved. When I couldn't hear anything, I slowly opened my eyes. The door stood open but Viola appeared to be gone. I pulled out of Julius' hold as he yanked the goggles off his head and covered his eyes with his hand. I was surprised he didn't swear.

"Fun isn't it?" I whispered. "Welcome to my world."

Patting his shoulder, I went into the wardrobe, thankful Viola hadn't found my hiding spot. Adjusting the belts, I hitched the pillow case over my shoulder.

"What's that?"

"Food and water." I glanced up at his shocked expression. "What? You really thought I was idle this entire time? And what's with the 'Baby' thing?"

"Code for new Nephilim. They're going to be swarming this place like ants."

"Won't the ice trick make us invisible?"

He shook his head. "Only when we're still. The light glints off me otherwise."

If light glinted, I couldn't understand how Viola hadn't seen us with the floodlight she'd used. She'd waved it around like a lightsaber. I had to trust him…for now. I didn't know if he was going to lead me down another rabbit warren-style wing like the infirmary to be bred…like…well, a rabbit, or if he would actually get me out of here. Grabbing Viola's camera, I slid the memory card into the coin pocket of the jeans then crept to the door and peered down the hallway. I was expecting half an army to be milling around like cops at a crime scene but the corridor was completely empty.

"You got a plan?" Julius was right behind me.

"Not really. You?"

"I had one, but it's not going to work now."

"All units, report in."

I nearly had heart failure at Viola's Apath then heard individual replies, all with negative responses.

"I have to report in." Julius told me.

"Won't that give away where we are?"

"One thing about Apath…" He grinned. "…you can't tell where it's coming from… *Julius. No sign.*"

"Okay, so one thing in our favour, they don't know where we are."

"That won't last long. They'll track you."

"How?"

"Petra."

That made sense. Petra was the wielder of the green glow. So it was a tracking ability.

"How long before she does that?"

"An average of twelve to fifteen minutes."

"That a guess?"

"Results of drills."

I retreated into the room. "Will they come back
here?"

"They shouldn't."

"In case they do, where is the best place to hide?"

"Against a visual check I'd hide on the roof above
your balcony."

Viola had left the window open so I hopped out
onto the ledge of the balcony. It was little wider than
a pot plant. Julius followed me out then pulled me
down into a crouch by my upper arms. He was so
close his breath was cold on my face.

"Nova, I don't think you understand the situation."

"I do. We hide here until Petra comes for me, then
we disable her."

"She won't physically come for you. She can find
someone by thinking about them."

"Just like Viola commands someone by speaking
words. I know."

"You're a sitting duck."

"Julius, I appreciate you wanting to help me. I
really do. But it might be best if you pretend like the
last fifteen minutes or so never happened and you
really don't know where I am. Go and be where
you're supposed to be."

"You'll never make it against thirty-three trained
Nephilim soldiers, pet."

"Thirty-two. You're on my side, right?"

He made a low growl in his throat then slammed
his mouth against mine without warning. For a few
seconds I was stunned. By the time I started
struggling he let me go.

"Your funeral, pet."

With that parting shot, he tossed the jacket in my direction and disappeared back through the window.

For a few moments shock shut down my brain before I realised how exposed I was and climbed the rough bricks to the roof line. I'd never gone rock climbing before. It was harder than it looked. Hiding in the shadows of a jutting piece of roof, I waited for Petra's glow to show, as I tried to figure out my next move.

If I could convince them I was already far away from here, I would have a fighting chance. Hopefully, it would mean they'd have fewer eyes keeping watch for me. I kept listening to the Apath reports. It was better than having an enemy radio unit. Concentrating, I broke etiquette and eavesdropped on the direct Apath, too. Well, I suppose I had a right…I was on the roof. With eaves. At first I thought it was weird that they Apathed everything, but then again, out of all of them it had only been Julius who habitually spoke to me verbally. I don't think I actually heard audible voices except in rare snatches since I got here.

Finally, I heard what I'd been waiting for.

"Petra. Find her."

"Yes, sir."

It only took a few seconds from the end of 'sir' for the green glow to show up. It looked more like laser light than glow as it came at me like an accusing finger. Staring directly at it I gave it the memorised longitude and latitude location. I had no idea if it would work. Like a blood hound, the ability might seek scent, if so, I was in trouble. The green stopped inches from me before its laser light intensity

softened into a haze, closer to the glow I'd come to
recognise. It hovered for a few heart beats, which
might not have been very long at all since my heart
was racing, then the glow pulled itself into a laser
again and shot off to my left.

"She's out of the compound." Petra announced.

"How the hell did she get that far?" Lauder
sounded furious.

"Scenario 'Fox Hunt' sir?" That was Viola.

*"Don't you think that's a little excessive,
sweetpea?"*

"Why? You got a soft spot for your little pet?"

"Authorised."

*"Lauder, I think this is like going after a mosquito
with a Gatling gun."*

*"I said authorised, Julius. If you want to question
it, you can stay here. In fact, that's a good idea."*

"Sir, I wasn't –."

*"Consider it a reprimand for the stunt you pulled
at the infirmary."*

That made me raise my eyebrows as I listened to
Viola give the Apath that 'Fox Hunt' was a go. I was
almost expecting to hear the words…'release the
hounds'. I had no idea what 'Fox Hunt' was but it
made me think of baying English hounds and
pounding horse hooves flinging mud divots in a spray
behind them. Add in a Nephilim or two and it
sounded like a horror story for me.

Climbing from the roof, I slipped on the last brick
and clumsily landed on the steel banister before
tumbling with a prat fall, onto the balcony and getting
knocked on the head by the pillow case of goodies. I
jarred my left hand which was still hurting from

Edward's grip, and my head was momentarily sore, but nothing new appeared to be damaged. My main concern was that anyone in the vicinity would have heard me. Nothing showed up on the Apath front and no one suddenly flung themselves out of the window to grab me, so after a few moments I calmed down and clambered back inside the room. Inching down the hallway, I slid my sunnies onto my head to take advantage of my night vision and slowly made my way through the house. I didn't need light to show me the place was deserted. That creeped me out. There had to be someone here. Hearing a low vibration, I frowned. I didn't think I'd heard that noise before but it sounded familiar. Seeing light beams cutting through the room, I slipped my sunnies back into place then sidled up to the nearest window.

Vehicles. A lemming line of them. They looked like armoured army jeeps of some kind. That was going to be real subtle when they hit a highway. Suddenly, I realised I was an idiot and began to crane my neck to see if I could figure where the vehicles were coming from. I couldn't see. I ran to the other window just in time to see the last vehicle drive up out of a rise in the ground before the ground lowered. Blinking, I moved my sunnies down my nose and stared. The ground was back to flat. If I hadn't seen it, I wouldn't have known it could move. Now I had to figure out how to get inside and see if there were any more vehicles. I hadn't seen the van, so there was some hope there.

What I really needed was a convenient computer left on with a program displaying blueprints of the building. That always happened in movies, right?

Since I didn't have a handy one of those laying around I headed off in the direction of the Thunder Bird-like garage. There had to be a door from the inside to access it.

Chapter Nineteen

I may not have found a convenient computer but I did find an emergency evacuation map near the fridge. I would have walked right passed it except I had a sudden image of Jason Bourne snatching one from the wall in the American embassy. I did the same.

I hadn't realised the kitchen pantry had a second exit, nor that it led to stairs. It was like walking into an entirely different world. One with bloody bright lights. No wonder the main house had low wattage lights. All the electricity was being syphoned down here for these ones. I also found where all the technology was. Pressed against the wall, I peered into a room that looked like a spaceship flight simulator. Hearing voices, I jerked back, then with a frown I peered around again. Voices?

Three guys, from the sound of it, were talking about a football game. Okay, maybe not so much the game as paying out on one of them for being a Collingwood supporter.

Crouching, I sidled around the corner and up to the door of the room. The three guys were on a mezzanine level behind glowing screens. There were definitely paying more attention to themselves than the screens and they all wore the same pale blue shirt and black pants. The shirts had the same logo.

Ibira Corp.

None of the three men had tells. After so long seeing tells on everyone I saw, it was a little disconcerting. As far as I knew, it meant only one thing. They were human.

Human security guards. That made about as much sense as goldfish guarding against sharks.

Keeping low, I snuck past the door, at any second expecting one of them to see me. The conversation continued without pause and I breathed a sigh of relief. My relief didn't last long. Hearing footsteps, I ducked into a narrow alcove and hid behind some neatly stacked pallet crates. A fourth human walked past. Wearing the same uniform as the others, he carried a tray of paper coffee cups. Just an ordinary day at the office. Hopefully it would remain that way for them as I made my escape.

I consulted the emergency map again. It showed more stairs further to the left but that's where I ran out of map. It was better than nothing and it gave me something to try for.

Standing from the crouch, I slid my hand up the wall as I peered above the crates, watching for movement and my hand encountered something cold and hard. It was a large, flat metal cabinet with a key in the lock. It looked similar to the fuse box on the roof at home. I glanced back down the hallway before I turned the key and swung the door open.

Eureka.

I wasn't an electrician by any stretch of the imagination but I'd queried the repair man when he'd come to the roof a few times. Plus, it helped that this fuse box was coded and the codes were explained in pencil on a chart set into the door. Hovering over the main power switch I changed my mind. I didn't want to rouse too much attention right away. Consulting the list I found the switches for the lights. I hit the safety switches for the common areas, there was a garage among them, and left the lights for the offices and named rooms on. I didn't know how to remove fuses and it would have look more suspicious anyway. Closing the door again, I locked it and pocketed the key before moving out of the alcove and heading for the stairs. Exiting the stairwell, I saw that the fuse box had obviously been for this level, too. According to the map, the garage was on this level. Right next to a guard station. There was also a smaller area behind the guard station labelled 'staff parking'. Keeping an eye out for guards roused by the garage suddenly plunging into darkness, I kept to the walls. It was huge. The floor was painted a light colour and it looked like the inside of what I'd imagine an aircraft hangar to look like. Exposed steel beams, pipes all over the place, and wide circular bulbs hanging from wires on the ceiling. The guard station was lit up like a Christmas tree but the one guard inside, also human, had his back turned and was playing a game on his phone. These guys were giving security guards a bad name. None of them appeared to be focusing on the job at hand. I suppose after months of watching over what amounted to a giant parking station, I'd be playing games on my phone, too. I didn't mind. It worked for me.

The back wall of the guard station had rows and rows of hooks. The ones over the label 'Hummers' were empty. The hooks over the label 'Vans' were still full as was 'Sedans' and 'Wagons'. I wasn't about to walk in there and tap the guy on the shoulder and ask him to move aside for a moment while I made my selection.

"Hey, Kevin. What's up?"

I nearly had heart failure as Julius appeared in the guard station from the other side.

"Nothing much. Had a flurry of activity a few moments ago. Do you know what that was about?"

"Nope, in the dark about that one."

Kevin placed his phone on the bench then turned back to Julius. It wasn't his phone that held my attention nor the packet of cigarettes. It was the car keys.

"Seems a little strange, being two in the morning and all."

"It's the Government, buddy. Maybe they're tracking aliens."

Kevin snorted. "Little green men like America, they don't often show their faces 'round here."

"Well, you know, one of them might have got himself a tourist visa."

Kevin tapped one of the computer monitors in front of him. "Stick around my friend and we can find out where the little tourist stranded himself."

Very, very carefully I reached into the room and swiped the keys. Jerking out of sight, I waited a moment for one of them to notice. Well, at least

Kevin didn't appear to notice and if Julius did, he wasn't giving me away.

Backtracking the way I came, I moved a distance away from the station before starting across the garage. It wasn't long before I came against row upon row of vans. They were black and they all had the Ibira Corp logo on the side. Subtle. Nothing screamed mysterious-bad-guys like a row of black vans. At the very end of the line were four white vans, naked of the logo. I paused. The interior of the van I'd been in had been pale. Like the other vans, these ones were unlocked. The first three were normal vans with seats all the way to the back. The fourth had one row of seats and what looked like racked shelves. I smiled as I saw a strap sticking out from the bottom of the shelves. Checking that the sliding door was unlocked, I very carefully slid it open far enough to clamber inside. It still made a loud metallic growl which echoed. I waited a moment or two, but saw no movement. The shelves were about ten centimetres deep but I knew the rest of the van was deeper than that. Placing my hand under the shelf, it suddenly lifted up in a noiselessly behind the shelves above, revealing an alcove fitted with the strapped bedding. I plunged my hand beneath and after a few moments of searching pulled out my phone. I had no idea why I'd wasted time on the task but there was something satisfying about retrieving my now dead and useless phone. After so long having everything I identified as me being stripped away I now had something of mine.

Retreating from the van I slowly shut the door again and turned. Gasping, I dropped to the floor, my

heart racing as I saw a figure leaning on the opposite
van in a relaxed cross-armed pose. Even with the
night vision goggles back in place, I recognised him a
split second later.

"Julius, you moron." I hissed at him.

He moved and dangled a set of keys from the
forefinger of his glove.

"You won't get far without these, pet." Julius'
voice sounded loud in the silence.

"Shh."

"Why? There's no one around to hear us."

"What about the guard?"

"Kevin?" Julius shrugged. "He's taking a well-
earned nap."

"Hibernation?"

"Possibly. I must admit I'm very impressed. I
don't know how you sent everyone off on a wild
goose chase, but it was beautiful."

He followed me as I started walking to where I
thought the staff garage should be. "Almost as
beautiful as you getting yourself left behind?"

"That wasn't part of the plan. You see, pet, I really
thought you'd somehow managed to pull something
off. You obviously had something up your sleeve…"
He waved a pointed finger at me. "…with your
provisions and everything, then suddenly being out of
the compound. It blew me away."

"So when did you figure I was still here?"

"When I saw you at the fuse box."

That shocked me. "You were randomly walking
past?"

"I was not so randomly checking the camera feeds to figure out how you'd slipped past everybody in such a short time."

"Cameras? Damn." I hadn't thought about that.

"There's none in the main house if that makes you feel better."

"Seriously? That's supposed to make me feel better? Are there any down here?"

He nodded. "Everywhere."

I froze, searching. "Hell."

"You do say that a lot."

"What do I do now?"

"I wouldn't worry…your stint at the fuse box may have put them out of order."

I frowned. "Nothing in that fuse box indicated cameras."

"No? Oh well, I must have got the idea to tamper with the fuse box for the cameras from you. Not so sure I would have thought about it otherwise."

"You must really get your jollies from messing with me." I glared at him as I started walking again.

"A man has to have a hobby. I'm curious though on what you plan to do next. Whose identifier code have you swiped? It'll have to be someone not already out there or it'll raise a red flag."

"Identifier code?"

"To open the garage door."

I smiled. "Yours."

He gave a slow smile in return. "What about Martin who checks visual identification at the inner gate post and Richard who does the same again at the boundary? Also, how do you plan to get around the tracker in every single one of these vehicles?"

I faltered and stared down at the keys I still held in my clenched hand. Action movies always made it appear easier than this. For every obstacle I figured out, there was another one ready to take its place. Frowning, I saw the logo on the keys then glanced at the black vans, an idea forming. It was crazy. Pure madness. It worked in the movies. Sure, with a stunt co-ordinator, stunt drivers and hours of prep time.

"Julius, you're the rebellious type right? Someone who might defy an order if it pissed you off enough?"

"What's on your mind, pet?"

"How wide are the back of those black vans? And are there portable ramps somewhere?" I held out my hand to show the keys. "We've got ourselves a Mini."

Chapter Twenty

Julius didn't call my idea ridiculous or tell me it was impossible. In fact, he seemed to be having fun as he reversed the van up to the older style Mini in the staff garage and set up the ramps. It was a tight fit but he impressed me with his driving ability. It took him a while to line the car up with the ramps but when it came to actually driving the car into the back of the van he made it look easy. The longer it took, the more concerned I became with someone discovering us. I didn't believe for a second that my stunt with Petra had completely cleared out the compound of Nephilim. I was also worried about what would happen when one of the guards reached for a light switch.

Julius scrambled though the sunroof of the Mini, and closed the rear doors before taking the driver's seat of the van. We were driving out of the staff garage when the lights came flooding on, momentarily blinding us both.

I shoved my glasses on as Julius yanked his goggles off. "I guess someone found the spare key to the fuse box."

"What about the cameras?"

"No one should realise they're not working for a little while yet."

"They'll have people watching them right? Like another guard station?"

His eyes seemed to adjust faster to the light than mine did and he started driving again. "An hour and a half. Should be another half hour or so before hibernation wears off."

"You like your party trick don't you?"

"I didn't want them seeing what I was looking for."

The first guard post was easy. Martin was human. I hid in the back of the van near the Mini. I could see Julius in the front of the van and I could just see Martin in the side mirror.

"Hey, Julius. I didn't realise you didn't go with that first group."

"Sure you did, Martin. You've got all the ins and outs recorded."

"True enough. ID and code please."

Julius pulled a plastic card from his pocket. "Nine-three-five-fourteen-one-fifteen."

"You meeting up with them?"

"Yep. Got the call to bring some equipment out."

"You ever going to tell me what you guys get up to?"

"You know that would mean I would have to kill you right, and you seem such a nice guy."

"Yeah, and my wife might complain about missing the pay cheque. You're clear, enjoy your night…or what's left of it."

"Sure thing."

I waited a little before moving up to the back of the seat. "He's human, right?"

"Yeah."

"Why do you have humans searching vehicles? A Nephilim would make more sense."

"Humans see things differently. Don't feel disappointed though. The next one is Nephilim. This is where it'll get tricky. Jump up front."

"Why?"

"Hiding in the back will seem suspicious."

I clambered over the front of the seat then slid my sunnies down my nose with a frown. The greyed vision showed me what I thought I saw. In a canopy covering the entire guard post, the gate and a good distance in front of us was a black glow. It moved and shimmered. First it was on our side of the fence, then swept to the far side, before returning in a sweeping arc back to our side. Don't ask me how I saw a black glow, but that's exactly what it was. We were still a ways off and I frantically tried to figure out what black meant. The darkest glow I'd seen so far had been…I moved in the seat until I could see my reflection in the side mirror.

Vision. Black could mean vision. Praying I was right, I took a breath and focused on the glow. The moment before Julius drove through the curtain of black I told it that it saw Julius alone in the van and that the back was shelves of equipment and tools. Kind of like a repairman's truck.

"Pretend I'm not here." I whispered to Julius as he drove closer.

"What? It won't work."

I didn't answer as Julius came to a halt at the gates. He chatted to Richard much like he'd done with Martin and my heart pounded the entire time, hoping like hell I'd been right. Black glowed from Richard's pupils like those old cartoon binoculars, starting small and growing bigger the further away from him it got. I realised the curtain I'd seen was the limit of his vision.

After a few minutes, he waved us through and we were on our way.

"Okay, you're going to tell me what the hell just happened back there." Julius told me after we'd driven out of sight of the gates.

"Nothing. He saw your ID, saw you and waved us though."

"Hogwash."

Surprised, I glanced at Julius. "For someone who plays at being the bad boy, you don't swear very well."

"Would you rather I said to cut the bullcrap?"

I shrugged. "It's a little better."

He pulled the van over in a cloud of dust on the side of the road.

"What are you doing?"

"I'm stopping right here, until you tell me what the hell it was you did."

"I didn't do anything. You saw me, I was sitting right next to you. I didn't move."

"Exactly. Richard can see through any invisibility or cloaking I have ever seen. He should have asked about you. He should have asked about the car in the back. Instead, he waved us through."

At least that confirmed that black did mean vision.

"I don't know what I did." I lied.

Julius shifted until he'd turned to face me on the bench seat, one hand on the steering wheel, one hand along the back of the seat. "You told me to pretend you weren't there. You knew he wouldn't see you."

"I didn't know that he wouldn't. I *hoped* that he wouldn't."

"Pretty big hope for someone who doesn't know what their ability is."

"It doesn't matter right? Soon I'll be out of your hair, and your conscience will be clear because you helped me." I swallowed hard as I looked across at him. The frost on his skin was moving like someone had shaken up a snow globe and his jaw was clenched like he was furious. I was so used to seeing him as easy going. The change made him look like one of those vigilante mercenary types. I flinched as he moved suddenly but all he did was slam the van into gear and spin the tyres in the dirt before shuddering us back onto the bitumen. I kept silent although I gripped the bar on the dash and the handle on the roof as he drove like a rally driver. A really angry rally driver.

After a few kilometres he calmed down…a bit. We drove along in silence without even the radio between us until he turned into pub-come-petrol station-come-convenience store. Nothing shouted rural country so much as one of these places. Julius pulled up near the back of the building, got out of the van then started working on removing the Mini from the back. I helped him with the ramps then stayed out of his way. He parked the little car as I shut the back doors on the van. I waited for a moment but he stayed near the other car. Hesitantly, I made my way over to him.

He didn't look at me as he pulled his hand from his pocket and pressed something into my hand that wasn't the keys.

"Some cash. It's not much. It'll keep you in gas for a little bit, but you're on your own after that."

"It's called petrol over here." I offered a small smile.

Finally, he looked at me. "I had hoped you'd trust me a little after all this time."

"I trust you a little, Julius, but you're still part of the crowd who kidnapped me."

There was silence for a moment then I held out my hand for the keys.

"Thank you for your help."

"Don't feel guilty, pet."

"About what?"

Without warning, he brought his hand to my head then kissed me. It wasn't a hard slam like before and it wasn't like the times he'd breathed cold air into my mouth. It was an honest to goodness kiss. Cold, but gentle…and a definite goodbye.

Slowly he pulled away and pressed the keys into my hand.

"Your boyfriend is one lucky man."

Stunned, I watched him walk over to the van, climb into the front, and pull out without so much as a backward glance. A few minutes later, I couldn't even see the van in the distance. I held my hand over my mouth trying to warm up my lips. For someone who couldn't manipulate my response, he did a pretty decent job at kissing. Even if it was cold. I snorted as

I dropped my hand. For someone who didn't actually have a boyfriend I was doing a decent job at getting kisses. With a sigh, I turned towards the front door of the establishment.

"Morning, love, you're out and about early. Don't often see bodies show up before the sun."

I smiled at the older lady. Her hair was a mess and she wore a robe pulled over a night dress. "Sorry. I'm a little lost. You see my phone died and I think I left my charger at the place I stayed last night. I was hoping someone had a charger I could borrow and a map maybe. I'm not sure exactly where I am."

"Where ya heading, love?"

"Melbourne."

"Well, you've got a ways yet, love. There's still a state and a half to go, but I can get ya that map. As for a charger, I don't have one for those newfangled phones meself but there should be something in the shop. You'll want a new one. I'll go open up for you. Do you want breakfast?"

"Sure. Can I use your facilities first?"

She handed me a key attached to a rubber thong. The footwear was grubby and missing great chunks out of it but I didn't complain. "Around the back, love, first door to the right."

Eden, as she told me her name was, seemed a friendly enough sort. She fixed a mean breakfast which I ate while I waited for the phone to charge. The location I'd sent the Nephilim was a middle-of-nowhere spot of bush about fifty kilometres north of us so I didn't panic. Once the phone was charged enough, I tried to call Zeph. It took me a moment to realise there was no reception.

"You don't have reception here?"

"Sorry, hon. You've got to hike it a fair way down Mossgiel til ya get to Hillston for reception. I do got a payphone."

I had never felt so much relief as the moment Zeph answered his phone.

"Zeph, it's Nova."

"Nova? Hey babe, how's the retreat going?" I frowned. I couldn't believe he'd fallen for the retreat crap. Before I could answer, he continued. "I'm glad you called actually, I found some of those coloured grade photo papers you like. I was going to get you some but I didn't know if you wanted red or green."

I held the phone away from my ear and stared at it, wondering if he'd suddenly gone mad. There was no such thing as coloured grade photo paper. Then it clicked. It had been forever since I'd even thought of the code stuff he'd drilled into me.

"Green's fine, Zeph, and as much of it as you like."

"Thank God. Hang on, I'm putting you on speaker. Where are you?"

"I'm in a pit stop in middle-of-nowhere New South Wales."

"New South Wales?" That was Tiberius. "No wonder we couldn't find you."

"What's the biggest town or city near you?" Zeph asked.

"Um…" I consulted the map again. "Griffith, I guess, maybe Hay."

"Hold on." Zeph told me and I heard a flurry of noise.

"What's happening?"

"Zeph's consulting." Benaiah told me and I smiled
at the sound of his voice. "Are you really okay?"

"Yeah. Just can't wait to be home."

"I can't zero in on you, only locations. " Zeph
sounded like he'd moved away from the phone, then
he was back. "Nova, can you get to Griffith?"

"Yes."

"Good. Find yourself a place to stay for a few
days, and let me know where it is."

"I've got some money but I don't think it'll cover
a few days."

"Can you get there on what you've got?"

"I think so."

"When you get there, have them ring me. I'll give
my credit card details…but, Nova?"

"Yeah."

"I'll expect you to pay me back so choose wisely."

I laughed. "Sure thing, Daddy."

Getting to Griffith was fairly easy. I followed
Mossgiel Trunk Road to Hillston, like Eden had told
me, then travelled the B87 or Kidman Way until I
reached it. The main problem was driving the Mini.
Kevin must have been one small guy. I wasn't a huge
person but it felt like I was driving with my knees
near my ears. I was so sore and stiff by the time I
started looking for a hotel. I didn't want to keep
driving in the small amount of traffic the town had, so
I pulled over at the first hotel I saw that looked like I
could afford it. I hadn't been active on any of my
websites for months. Sales were going to be down.
The staff of the hotel seemed friendly, the rooms were
fairly cheap and surprisingly spacious, even if it
looked like it had been thirty years since the place had

been last renovated. It had really good food though,
and that nearly made up for the traffic, night club
atmosphere of the street and the trains which kept me
up most of the night. Not that the bright lights let me
get much sleep in the first place. If I wasn't in my
room, I spent most of my time in the town library
which was practically next door. I hoped Zeph wasn't
going to take too long getting here. I was looking
forward to a full night of uninterrupted sleep.

Chapter Twenty One

I jerked out of the sleep I'd finally managed to settle into. The entire place was lit up and people were running around outside everywhere.

"Emergency evacuation. Please evacuate your rooms."

It wasn't the sound of the evacuation that had me up and racing to the bathroom for my clothes, it was the sound of Apath. I grabbed my underwear, grimacing…they were still damp from when I'd washed them out last night. I pulled them on all the same. Shoving my jeans on, I yanked my shirt over my head and grabbed my jacket. Turning, I almost had heart failure when Zeph burst through the wall.

He shimmered. "Nova. Thank God. Don't go out there and for God's sake don't Apath."

"Nephilim."

"Swarming the place like a SWAT team. You took a Mini didn't you?"

"Yeah. How did you—?"

"They found it. Grab your stuff. We need to get out of here."

Shoving the damp socks into my pocket, I pulled on the boots, yanked the laces tight, grabbed my phone, the charger and the small amount of change I had left. Taking a second to make sure I still had the memory card from Viola's camera, I pushed my sunnies into place and pulled my jacket on.

"Okay. Let's go."

"That's it?"

"Yeah, why?"

"That was quick."

"Are you going to complain or are we going to move?"

"Not complaining." He said as he came close to me. He wrapped his arms around me as his wings came around us like a cocoon.

"Don't be afraid…and you might want to close your eyes."

He shimmered and I felt my stomach lurch. I hurriedly obeyed him when I saw we were heading for the ceiling. When I felt breeze, I opened my eyes. We were above the hotel. Through his wings, I could see people congregating on the street and Nephilim going in and out of buildings. I saw Petra's green glow arching up from her and craned my neck to see where it ended. I looked down and saw her laser light heading directly for us. I saw Viola as Zeph climbed higher. Taking a breath, I told the glow that Viola was me. The laser softened like last time, then arched like an Olympic diver and headed directly for her. I didn't see what happened after that. The streets became light-filled rivers which fell away behind us.

Zeph's arms weren't that tight around me and I could feel a cushion of air beneath my feet and wrapping around me. I saw that I was pretty much standing on the bottom-most tips of his wings and I was leaning against the rest of them. Surprisingly, he didn't actually use his wings to fly like I thought he would. It was the most amazing feeling. I'd always wanted to try gliding. This was what I'd imagine it to be like.

"Can you hear me?" I asked him above the wind.

"Yes."

"I thought you couldn't talk when you're invisible."

"No one can hear me unless I'm flying with them."

"Zeph?"

"Hmmm."

"This is seriously cool."

He laughed. "Really? You're not scared?"

"I can see your wings. They're kind of like a translucent safety net."

"Good."

"How high can you go?"

"About ten thousand feet."

"Have you tried higher?"

"Yes. Despite being Nephilim I do need the basics…like…I don't know, air."

I looked down at the ground below. I could see the land, the trees and a river

"How are you navigating?"

"I can feel the magnetic pull of the earth."

"How did you find out you could fly?"

"I fell out of a four-story window."

"So if you weren't Nephilim, you'd pretty much be dead now."

"Yes. If Benny wasn't my brother, I'd be dead a thousand times over."

"He doesn't like the name Benny, you know?"

"I know."

"Why do you call him that then?"

"I'm his baby brother. I'm supposed to be annoying."

"How come you tease him about his lack of a love life when you know he's an untouchable?"

"What is this? Twenty questions?"

"Well, you don't have a radio."

"I'll get right on that. Look, Nova…" I winced. I really did hate people who started a sentence with 'Look'. I thought it was arrogant and rude. "…I know my brother, okay? I know that life is never going to be easy for him. But I also know that he's painfully shy and awkward. If I let him travel the path he wants, he'll end up as the male equivalent of the cat lady. Okay, so he'll never have a family but he can have friends. If I don't push him, he'll hide himself away forever. Besides which…I don't like cats."

I gave the laugh he was expecting. "I suppose it makes sense. I'm not so sure that you're doing it the best way."

"It's the only way I've got and I'm not going to stop. Never in a million years. You hear me?"

"I hear you."

"Good."

Zeph needed to stop every two hours or so and he needed sleep after about six. We made it to Cobram that first night and Wallan the next. We were so close to home, but I didn't push him. I knew how exhausted I'd been after two hours on a treadmill. This had to be worse. He wanted to wait until after dark before the final leg of the journey, and it was a little after nine according to the watch on his wrist when he finally touched down on the roof of our building. Benaiah was pacing and Zeph laughed behind me. He shimmered.

"Stress less, Benny, she's safe and sound."

Benaiah spun toward us and took a few steps before coming to a standstill. I wasn't having any of it. I ran right up to him and gave him a huge hug. I lay my head against his shoulder as his arms came around me.

"Don't mind me." Zeph said behind us. "I'm just the taxi."

I pulled away from Benaiah and gave Zeph a hug, too. "Thank you so much, Zeph. For everything."

"You're welcome. Glad to see you home. Be gentle with him. I think you gave him grey hairs."

With that parting shot, Zeph left Benaiah and me alone on the roof.

"Hi." He smiled.

"Hi, back at you."

"Nova…" He sighed. To my surprise, he closed the gap between us and placed his hands on the sides of my face.

"I'm pretty exhausted, you know. I could drain you."

"You've also got a hairline fracture in your left hand, that'll drain me faster." He didn't move his hands away.

"It's broken?"

"Not for long."

"It didn't hurt that much."

His eyes searched my face. "I'm relieved that you're okay."

"I am, too. Believe me."

"I am so sorry." He whispered, placing his forehead against mine.

I was completely bewildered. "What for?"

"That day in your office. You scared the hell out of me by telling me you liked me, too. I've spent my life staying away from people. I don't know how to do relationships."

"It's okay. We'll figure it out."

"Nova…"

"Yes, Benaiah?" I prompted when he fell silent and a blush stole over his cheeks.

"May I kiss you?"

I felt the tension inside me release. It was so nice to be *asked* for a kiss. "Yes, please."

His lips were gentle, hesitant, and warm. He wasn't confident and he didn't just take. It was the sweetest kiss I'd ever had. Taking in a slow breath, I told his rainbow to lift a tissue thin distance from me.

Benaiah gasped and his eyes opened. "I'm not healing."

"Shhh." I placed a finger on his lips. "I know."

Leaning in, I placed my mouth against his again. This time his hands slid under my jacket and he pulled me closer. Lost in the kiss, my hold on his rainbow slipped and he rocked a little before lifting his head.

"Wow. I think I need to sit down."

Laughing, I sat next to him on the bench and he took my hand in his. His rainbow sank into my skin and I let it.

"I've never felt that before." He told me.

"You've never kissed someone before either."

"I have actually. It didn't end well."

"If that was the case, why did you kiss me?"

He stared at our hands and blushed. "I'd spent so long thinking I'd lost you. I needed to let you know…that I want, I guess…more than I've ever had with anyone else. I don't know how, and I know it'll be hard, but I want to try."

"That was me by the way."

He laughed. "I didn't think I was kissing someone else."

"No, I meant, that moment when you weren't healing, that was me. That's my ability, I can affect other people's abilities. I guess I need more practice."

A slow grin crossed his face accompanied with another blush. "I'm willing to help you practice."

I hit his arm lightly then settled into his embrace. I watched his rainbow for a while.

"What happens when you run out of things to heal?"

"What do you mean?"

"My hand's no longer broken and I don't feel exhausted any more…"

"Elasticity in your skin, dying cells, dying hair follicles, pollutants in your lungs, worn down cartilage, cholesterol, the beginning of a resistance to your own insulin …there is always something to heal."

My eyebrows lifted. "I have all that?"

"And more. What you no longer have is the war of the cells. You are completely Nephilim now."

*****

Kate and Clancy were pleased to see me. Thanks to Benaiah, I just looked as if I'd gone on a decent holiday and Kate was more upset that I hadn't brought presents back than the fact I'd been gone for two and a half months. Needless to say, they were absolutely thrilled that Benaiah and I were officially an item…as they always knew we were.

I asked Tiberius to remove his illusion from around my eyes and found it amusing that he'd forgotten he'd done it. Life was slowly getting back to normal. Well, as normal as it would get for me at any rate. I eventually found a glare shield for my computer screen that worked as long as I wore my sunnies at the same time. It meant I could work on my blog and website gallery, getting back to promoting my photos and creating covers and swag for authors.

As for photography, well, I still had a way to go. Falling back onto the basic training of taking a photo on auto and recording the levels and trying to mimic the photo on manual, I was slowly teaching myself the difference between what I saw and what the camera saw. Baby steps were so frustrating when I was so used to flying.

"Nova, please."

"No."

"Why not?"

I pointed to my sunglasses. "Photophobic eyes, remember."

"That doesn't mean you can't come to the movies with me."

"Actually, it does."

"But you watch movies all the time."

"I used to watch movies all the time. Now I have to settle for DVD or download with the light balances in the room similar to the movie. Not something I can achieve in a cinema."

"You and Ben never go out."

"We went to the museum the other day."

It was actually a big step for Benaiah to go out in a crowd like he had, but it had been cold enough for him to wear gloves.

"Museum? Pft. You sound like an old married couple."

"And you sound like a petulant teenager."

"We could go shopping?"

"Good idea. We need more food in the house."

"Not food shopping, idiot. Clothes shopping."

"I have enough clothes."

"Well, window shopping then."

"I certainly don't need any new windows."

Kate stuck her tongue out at me. "Ever since you came back from the retreat you've been worse with your camera than you ever were before."

"Nope…" I mused. "…don't think it's possible."

Giving a frustrated growl, Kate bounced around my bed until she was sitting with her legs crossed. "So what are you going to do today?"

"I was going to make some batches for Mrs K and the rest."

"I thought you said we didn't have any food."

"I said we needed more food."

"Having a boyfriend was supposed to make you more fun, not more of a stick in the mud."

"I love you, too, Kate."

"You're my favourite stick in the mud though."

"Glad to hear it."

Finally, Kate left the room and I could finish getting dressed. It was such a relief to have nothing but jeans and slacks to choose from. Standing in the kitchen, I tied on my apron to start on the food and saw the over flowing bin. I gave a sigh and checked the cleaning roster even though I knew whose week it was.

"Kate, can you empty the bin please?" I yelled out.

"I'm in the bath."

"Of course you are." I muttered. Undoing the apron again I grabbed a second bag and picked up all the rubbish from the floor and out of the top of the bin. When I could manoeuvre the bin without it spilling everywhere, I tied the two bags, relined the bin, then headed off downstairs with both hands full. Tossing the bags into the dumpster I turned around and backed up with a small scream. Heart pounding, I took in the Nephilim in front of me. He was glowing white so much his clothes looked white. He also had wings. They were bigger and more solid looking than Zeph's.

"Don't be scardy, Missy Quinn."

"Mr Wendel?" Mr Wendel was Nephilim? Far out. "Oh my goodness, I didn't realise it was you. It's been a while."

"Long time, short time. Who is right to measure time?"

"No one, I guess. How have you been?"

"Not so bad, not so good." He twisted his hands together and took a step closer. "Help, Missy Quinn?"

I wasn't expecting that. He'd never asked for help specifically before. "Are you asking for help? Or offering to help?"

"Both." He shuffled back and forth.

"What do you need, Mr Wendel?"

"To help…help…help, Missy Quinn. I have to help, I have to…it's the only way you see. But you don't see. No one sees. All you have to do is help. Other people. Help. It's always about other people."

That wasn't confusing at all. "I'm sorry, Mr Wendel, I don't understand."

He looked down at his hand in his grotty glove then held it out like a kid proving he'd washed his hands. Palm up, fingers wide.

"Helping hand, Missy Quinn. I've got two. Only two. Needs a healer, tinker, tailor…doesn't want a candle maker. Bones are sore." He began to make a sound which could have been a demented donkey.

"Saw? Sore bones…?" Suddenly I got it. "You need a doctor. Mr Wendel, do you need a doctor?"

"Not me. Him."

He pointed to a lump of stuff by the dumpster. I crept closer. After a moment, I saw it was human. A human curled up in a foetal position. The hair was absolutely filthy and the clothes were as bad as Mr Wendel's.

"Is he your friend, Mr Wendel?" I glanced up at him, but he'd gone. I looked back down at the ragamuffin man. It was a man. He had a beard. My stomach roiled but I pushed the hair away from his face and saw the matted blood from his nose and mouth.

"Benaiah." I direct Apathed. *"I need you. Near the bins."*

I didn't get a returned Apath but a few minutes later, Benaiah burst from the front doors.

"Over here." I called. "I didn't know what else to do."

Benaiah looked down at him then crouched at his side. "It's okay."

He touched the man's face and I saw the rainbow sink down into his skin. Suddenly, Benaiah gasped and jerked his hand back.

"He's been injected with Nephilim gene. A few days ago, a week, maybe. The war of the cells has already started. What's he doing here?"

"Mr Wendel brought him to me. He thought I could take him to a doctor."

"Mr Wendel?"

"A homeless guy I know."

Suddenly, my hand was gripped and the injured man pulled me down. "Nova, help…please."

I gasped in shock as I stared down at him. "Oh, hell."

"Nova? What's wrong?"

"It's Edward."

To be continued…

Sneak Peek

Nephilim Code
Edward

"Why are you in Melbourne, Edward?"

I crossed my arms then leaned on the counter. Lowered pose. Confidence from a non-dominate stance. It annoyed the hell out of everyone. "Went through my wallet. Clever."

"What makes you say that?" The taller of the two asked.

"Address, name. What else did you find out? I'm dying to know."

"Arrogant," the bulky one muttered.

"Thick." The taller one tapped his head.

I straightened as he walked away from the counter. Seconds later he disappeared, making me jump when he appeared next to me.

"So Edward Huber, when did you decide we were human?"

Nephilim. Enemy camp. "Fu –."

"No you don't," the bulky guy said.

"We're good wholesome boys," the taller one told me. "Don't appreciate that word. Plenty of others for you to use."

I ran my mind through anyone I knew who manifested invisibility. Particularly from the other side. I came up empty.

"Who are you?"

The taller one reached across and held out his hand. "Zeph Anglelis."

I didn't shake it as my mind clicked. Zeph Angelis, brother of… "You're Benaiah Angelis?"

The bulky one lifted a hand in acknowledgement.

Benaiah Angelis. The one Nephilim Lauder wanted. The one Nephilim who had slipped from his grasp. The only Nephilim in recorded history who could heal. I was in the same room as Benaiah Angelis.

"Figures." Zeph pushed away from the counter. "He knows who you are."

"Not really an accolade," Benaiah told him.

"True. But he still hasn't answered the question."

I looked down at my hands. He'd touched my wrist. I had been healed by Benaiah Angelis. "That's why I feel better."

"Not even a thank you. Did you notice?" Zeph was back to talking with his brother.

"I noticed."

"Thank you," I said automatically.

"Well, what do you know? The brat has manners."

Zeph was really on my nerves.

"I can't tell you."

"You can't tell us what?" Zeph turned back to me.

I glared at him. He was damn pushy. I glanced at Benaiah. He seemed to be waiting.

"I can't tell you why I'm in Melbourne."

"Really? How odd."

I wanted stinging serum. Thirty milligrams. He would go down for hours. I tensed my hand. Waiting for the slide. Nothing. I pushed away from the counter. I didn't care if they didn't like the word. I told Zeph what he could do with himself.

Zeph smiled. "Flattered but no thanks. I'm not my type."

"Please don't use that word Edward." Benaiah's tone was all 'Mum' again but I swallowed in guilt.

No one requested with a 'please'. At least not to me.

"Whatever. Believe what you want."

"What happened? They put a blindfold on you, spun you three times, and you suddenly found yourself here?" Zeph snorted.

"You won't believe me so what's the point?"

"Try."

I frowned. Benaiah's softly spoken 'try' twinged a memory. I couldn't grasp it. It was buried beneath too much pain.

"I'm human." I waited for shock. Surprise. A response of any kind. Nothing. "What no gloating?"

"Why would we gloat?" Benaiah asked with a slight shrug.

"Not even you?"

Zeph lifted his hands in surrender. "Dude, that's your battle."

These guys were weird.

"Lauder figured I was as good a test subject as any. I didn't argue. If it worked, I was back in the game."

"It didn't work," Benaiah said quietly. It wasn't a question.

I clenched my teeth. I had wanted it to work. I was convinced it would work. I swallowed hard, took a breath and got the rest of the story out as quickly as possible. "I got sick like the others. Lauder kicked me out. Said I was useless."

Again nothing. No agreement with the decree. No snide remarks. These guys didn't know a door of kick-him-when-he's-down opportunity when it stood wide open in front of them.

"So how'd you get here?"

And there it was. Of course Zeph wanted the degrading details.

"Hitched a ride or two, walked when I couldn't. Begged for food, stole money. Then I got sicker, I remember that. I couldn't move. Could barely breathe. There was this crazy guy. Super demented in the head. And…" I struggled to remember anything else, but drew a blank. "…then I woke up here."

I waited. The brothers were silent. Probably Apathing.

Finally Zeph moved. "Do you believe him?"

"Sounds genuine."

"Could be a trap."

"Could be."

"Wait for the others?"

Benaiah nodded. "Yes."

"Others?"

On cue a knock came at the door. Ignoring me Zeph went to answer. Racing around I reached the door before him and blocked it.

"What others?"

"Nephilim."

"No you don't. I want to know who they are first."

"Why? Want to know how many have it in for you?" Zeph grabbed my arm.

I shoved a hand against his chest, pushing him away. Backing up I was determined to stay put. Suddenly I felt myself falling. I was sitting on the floor of the hallway. My legs through the door. Fear raced through me. I scrambled backwards.

"Well that's not something you see every day." A very British accent announced.

I looked up at the Nephilim. I looked at the door. The closed door.

"What the hell just happened?"